SECONDS TILL SLAUGHTER . . .

Reno pulled the hammer back and moved the front sight to center on the leading rider. He had a rifle across his thighs—and barely a minute to live.

The wagon reached the little pyramid of rocks. A fusillade of shots swept the driver off the seat and the riders out of their saddles. Reno fired at the near horse. The wagon smashed into it, heaved up on its side, and turned over.

Suddenly everything was still; the firing stopped.

Nate said loudly, "That's all of 'em."

DON'T MISS THESE
ALL-ACTION WESTERN SERIES
FROM THE BERKLEY PUBLISHING GROUP

THE GUNSMITH by J. R. Roberts
>Clint Adams was a legend among lawmen, outlaws, and ladies. They called him . . . the Gunsmith.

LONGARM by Tabor Evans
>The popular long-running series about U.S. Deputy Marshal Long—his life, his loves, his fight for justice.

LONE STAR by Wesley Ellis
>The blazing adventures of Jessica Starbuck and the martial arts master, Ki. Over eight million copies in print.

SLOCUM by Jake Logan
>Today's longest-running action Western. John Slocum rides a deadly trail of hot blood and cold steel.

•·◆ WESLEY ELLIS ◆·•

LONE STAR

AND THE DEATH CHASE

J
JOVE BOOKS, NEW YORK

LONE STAR AND THE DEATH CHASE

A Jove Book / published by arrangement with
the author

PRINTING HISTORY
Jove edition / February 1994

ISBN: 0-515-11314-X

A JOVE BOOK®
Jove Books are published by The Berkley Publishing Group,
200 Madison Avenue, New York, New York 10016.
JOVE and the "J" design are trademarks belonging to Jove Publications, Inc.

PRINTED IN THE UNITED STATES OF AMERICA

10 9 8 7 6 5 4 3 2 1

★
Chapter 1

The dusty wagon train, sixteen wagons pulled by mules, slowly snaked its way into the narrow valley, following the old post road. It was two hours past midday and hot, not a cloud in the high sky. A few hawks circled over the brown hills as lazy plumes of dust curled up from the wagon wheels and the hoofs of the riders and drifted off to the south.

The wagon master, Jed Fellowes, squinted at the closing slopes, wishing he had insisted they take the southern route over the plains where there were no encircling hills. He had fought Indians in his day, and roads and trails through narrow valleys always made him nervous—not to be able to see for miles around. The other route was longer and would probably have added a day's travel, but in his opinion it was much safer. He would cheerfully exchange time for safety. One of these days he would retire to a rocking chair on a porch somewhere, and he would like it to be without bullet holes in his skin.

He reined in and looked along the curving line of wagons. All were moving steadily, mules' heads bobbing and nodding as they plodded, wagons creaking . . . A couple more days and they would be in Ebanville. He'd let them all rest up a day and do a little repair work when they got there. If he remembered, there was a hurdy-gurdy dance house in the town, and he smiled at the sky, thinking about the girls.

But they weren't there yet. He turned the roan horse, and his gaze swept along the hills to the north—they were the closest—and he stiffened. A sudden flash of light—was it a reflection from bright steel in a cleft of the hills? He spurred the roan and yelled to George Minz, the nearest horseman, telling him to alert the others.

Minz stared at him in surprise—then the first shots came! Riders pounded down the steep slope toward them, seeming to rise from the ground! Jed yanked out his rifle, levered it, and fired, all in one quick motion. He fired twice more—then his horse was hit and went down, legs kicking wildly. Jed rolled free and lay on his belly, firing again at the charging men.

The raiders were at the wagons, and Jed struggled to get up and fell heavily. He had been hit just below the knee. In the excitement he had felt only a blow, and now it began to hurt. His leg was all bloody. Whipping out his knife, he cut away the jeans to expose an ugly wound. He wrapped it as well as he could to staunch the blood . . .

He was lying in a slight hollow, too far distant to see clearly what was happening at the wagons. The firing had stopped and men were moving about—it was difficult to hold his head up to see. The leg hurt like blue blazes, and he hugged it and lay back, staring at the sky, feeling helpless.

After a bit the bleeding stopped and he was thirsty. There was a canteen on the dead horse; he scurried around and inched toward it.

As he reached it, two horsemen galloped toward him and he drew his revolver, yanking back the hammer. He'd get

2

one of them before— Then he saw that one of the riders was George Minz! He put the gun away and laid his head on the sand, dead tired.

They carried him back to the wagons and laid him in the shade. Someone worked over his wound while he drank whiskey to dull the pain. The raiders had shot the lead mules, George told him, halting the wagons. Then they had been robbed. No one had been killed, but three were wounded, two slightly. They were bandaged and lying in the wagons.

"They wanted money," George said. "Made us all turn out our pockets. Then they went through the wagons, five of them. They called the leader Reno."

"Reno . . ." Jed said. "I heard that name before—think I seen it on a poster."

"Yeah, I seen one, too," Minz said. "That jasper is wanted for murder and robbery. Mean as a snake."

Jessie Starbuck and Ki were in Ebanville when the wagon train arrived and made camp just outside town. The local doctor had the wounded men taken to his office immediately. He rebandaged the two slightly hurt men and sent them on their way. A third man, badly wounded, and Jed Fellowes were put into a spare room, and the doctor worked over them for several hours.

The arrival of the battered wagons caused much talk in the saloons, and the name of the bandit leader, Reno, was on all lips. The sheriff had his deputy rustle through a stack of wanted fliers and tack up several with Reno's reward prominent. The bandit was worth one thousand dollars to the man who brought him in, dead or alive. The others of his gang were worth five hundred each.

It was a handsome offer, for Reno, but no one rushed out and jumped on his horse to chase after. Reno was dangerous and very sudden.

Jessie and Ki sat with Deputy U.S. Marshal Scott Pelter in the back room of the Nugget Saloon, seated around a green-topped card table. As Pelter said: "We've been after Reno—his name is Reno Quant—for two years or more on murder charges. He gunned down a federal judge while making an escape from a jail in Missouri."

"And now he has a gang," Ki said. "Five men, they say, all told."

"Yes. They've been running together for quite a while. We know their names and we have partial descriptions." Pelter looked at Jessie. "Are you going to interest yourselves in this affair?"

She glanced at Ki and shook her head. "We're on our way to San Francisco, as you know. We'll be on the next stage."

Pelter nodded as Ki rose. He said, "I want to see the stableman before he hits the hay." He went out and closed the door.

Pelter reached out for her hand. "I'm going to be very sorry you've gone. You've made these few days we've had together something I'll never forget . . ."

She smiled. "I won't forget them either, Scott. I'm sorry . . . that things . . . come between us."

He brightened. "But we can have one last night together."

She squeezed his hand. "Come to my room at nine . . ."

Scott Pelter was a young man, nearing thirty, well set up, with broad shoulders and narrow hips—something like Ki, Jessie thought, but with blondish hair instead of black, and a rather square face that smiled easily. He had been attentive from their first meeting, and they had spent several joyous nights together. She regretted they would soon come to an end.

She and Ki had been in communication with an attorney

4

in San Francisco who was eager for them to come and get to the bottom of a local scandal. The attorney was a friend, and Jessie wanted to help . . .

Scott was on time, finding the door ajar. He slipped inside and bolted it. They had conducted themselves judiciously; there had been no gossip flowing from their trysts. Scott was not married and did not drink; he had not mentioned to a soul that he was intimate with the green-eyed, honey-blond vision that all men hungered after upon seeing her on the streets.

He took her in his arms at once, kissing her with a kind of desperation, till she laughed and pushed him away, coming up for air. "Let me breathe!"

He scooped her up and carried her to the wide bed. Head and foot it had iron curlicues that someone had painted white. She pointed to a table where she had bottles and glasses set out. "Wouldn't you like a—"

"I would like *you*!" He picked at her clothes. "Our time together is slipping away."

She could not deny that. They made a game of undressing each other, though he pulled her clothes off faster, and when she was naked, she rolled to the center of the bed and watched him push off his boots and jeans and nearly tear the shirt from his back in his haste.

Then he jumped on the bed and embraced her, and they rolled from one side to the other, laughing and kissing wildly.

And somewhere in their wrestling, his hard member managed to find its way into her eager nook. Her legs slid around him, and for a short, frantic while they were in their own tiny world, struggling toward release—which came too soon. She cried out softly as the incredible sensations twisted her, feeling him panting and thrusting madly of a sudden, and then moaning, kissing her neck as he jerked and gradually subsided . . .

•   •   •

In the morning, when she woke, he was gone. He never stayed to risk, in the hallways, the stares of early risers.

She met Ki downstairs in the hotel dining room. He was dressed as usual in a loose cotton shirt, leather vest, and black jeans that very obviously contained muscle. He moved like a panther, and looked something like an Indian, which he was not. Others in the restaurant thought he might be Chinese, but he was not that either. When questioned he admitted to being half-Japanese.

And he had interesting news.

"There was another man with the wagon master who was treated by the doctor here in town."

From Ki's tone Jessie knew he was saying something important. "What is it?"

"The other man was Professor Jeff McCook—you remember him?"

"McCook! Of course! He was with my father in China, helping to excavate some tombs and ancient buildings. That was a long time ago . . ."

"Well, he's here, in the doctor's care."

"What in the world is he doing in this part of the country?"

Ki shrugged. "From what they tell me, he was interested in some Indian diggings. You can see him anytime . . ." He looked at his watch. "It's early. Let's have breakfast first. McCook is probably still asleep."

"Oh, I'll be so glad to see him again! We've so many things to talk about. Was he badly wounded in the attack?"

"I'm afraid so. And he's getting on in years . . ."

Jessie toyed with a fork. "He was shot by that man, Reno . . . for a few dollars . . ."

"Yes." Ki looked at her. "Are you thinking what I think you're thinking?"

She nodded, frowning. "You know I am."

• • •

6

Dr. Amos Carr's shingle was nailed to a post near his mailbox in front of a red brick house with vines creeping over it. Ki used the black iron knocker on the door, and it was opened by a stout woman who asked their business.

Jessie said, "We've come to ask about Professor McCook."

The woman invited them in and pointed to a row of chairs in the hall. "I'll get the doctor for you."

"Thank you."

The wide hall led from the front door to the back of the house, where some kind of bustle was going on. Jessie could see several men coming and going past a half-open door. Then they carried something outside and the door slammed. In a few minutes the doctor came toward them, removing his spectacles, smiling to see a beautiful woman waiting to talk to him. "I'm Dr. Carr . . ."

Jessie said, "You have a patient named McCook?"

He sighed. "I did, miss. Yes."

"What d'you mean?"

Carr motioned toward the back. "Mr. Leech, the undertaker, is moving the body out now. Professor McCook died in the night, I'm sorry to have to tell you. Were you friends of his?"

Jessie nodded, biting her lower lip.

Ki said, "The gunshot wound was—"

"There was no way to remove the bullet without killing him on the table. No matter what, I'm afraid it was only a question of time. He could not be saved." The doctor shook his head. "Sometimes I am helpless . . ."

Chapter 2

Over supper in the hotel, Jessie said, "Can we postpone the trip to San Francisco?"

"Of course." Ki smiled. "You hadn't seen the professor for a long, long time . . ."

"Maybe not, but he was a close friend of Father's, and he was killed by a damned bandit. I don't have to like it."

Ki's brows rose a fraction. Jessie seldom swore. It showed how deeply she felt about McCook's death. It was almost as if the bandit had shot her father, Alex Starbuck, himself.

He said, "Then let's talk to Scott Pelter and see what his office has on Reno. They've been after him for a long time. They may know quite a bit."

"Yes, they should." She was silent a moment. "Are you with me in this?"

Ki looked astonished.

She said hurriedly, "I'm sorry—I didn't say that."

They went to Scott Pelter's office, and he was delighted to learn Jessie was not going to San Francisco after all. But he was more surprised to hear her say she and Ki were determined to go after the bandit Reno Quant.

It was a square office, paneled in wood, over the bank building. He motioned them to chairs and sat behind the wide desk, saying he had misgivings about that plan. "I know your reputation, and Ki's, of course, but they are five to your two."

"We've faced odds before. What do you know about Quant?"

"A great deal," Scott said. He paused. "Let me rephrase that. We *think* we know a great deal about him. He is wily and clever as a Sioux, very smart. By the way, the attack on the wagon train seemed to me a chance thing, as if the gang came upon the train unexpectedly. It wasn't well planned."

Ki said, "It came off well—for them."

"Yes, well, they're experienced robbers and killers. I'm surprised they didn't ambush the train instead of swooping down on it as they did." He shrugged. "But that's all speculation. To continue—we think Reno goes east in the wintertime, because we have no record or report of his doings during those months for several years."

Jessie nodded. "So he spends his money in the east—do you have any idea where?"

The deputy marshal shook his head. "None at all. It is my belief that when he boards a train heading east—or perhaps south—he assumes another identity."

"That's likely," Jessie said. Then she asked, "What about the other four members of the gang? Do they follow him east?"

"We don't know, but I would assume so. Either that or they hole up somewhere for the cold months. It's a fair-weather gang, you might say."

Ki asked, "How long has the gang been together?"

"For about four years, we think." Scott stressed the "think." "As you might expect, it's difficult to be certain

9

of anything concerning the Quant gang. They are good at leading false trails."

"What about favorite hangouts?"

"We know about several," Scott said, surprising them. He turned to a large map of the territory tacked to the wall. "One is here at Korning, and another at a little burg called Landers. Both are out-of-the-way places and probably lawless to boot. We know of them through informers who tell us Reno and his men have been seen there often after a job, spending money freely. He is cock of the walk, of course, when he shows up. And by the way, he is a heavy gambler."

Scott handed Jessie a sheet of foolscap. "Here are their names, with a brief description of each." He shrugged. "I know it's not much, but it's all we have."

She read the list quickly. Reno Quant, Nate Tupper, Sonny Ruff, Vince Seeley, and Gage Hindman. She handed the paper to Ki and studied the map. "Both towns are north of here. Maybe they're going to one of them . . ."

"It's possible, of course. When they left the wagon train, they pointed west, but that means nothing. Out of sight, they could have gone in any direction."

Ki said, "No one tried to track them?"

Scott shrugged again. "There was no tracker at the scene. By the time we could get one there, it was probably too late."

Ki nodded, but he had doubts about that. Five horses would leave a rather plain trail—unless a high wind got at it, with a bit of rain.

Scott said, "There's been talk about bringing in the Army to help round them up, but I'm afraid the Army would do more harm than good. They are not trained to hunt down criminals." He looked at them, frowning. "Are you two sure you want to take this on?"

"Positive," Jessie said, and Ki nodded.

• • • •

It was definitely their last night together—for a while at least. She and Ki had decided to go north in the morning, heading for Korning, the nearest of the two outlaw towns.

A single candle was burning on the far side of the room, a tiny spear of light nearly overwhelmed by shadows. They lay naked on the bed, and Scott kissed her hungrily, her neck and breasts, teasing the hard nipples as she squirmed in the near dark. His erection rubbed along her thigh, and she captured it, holding it with both hands, nipping at his earlobe. They writhed together; he reveled in the feel of her warm, silky skin, and he rolled, pulling her atop him for a moment. Her blond hair cascaded over his face, and she laughed, tossing her head, moving so her full breasts caressed his lips. Then he rolled her onto her back and slid between her luscious thighs . . .

"Now—" she whispered, guiding his taut member to its nest. He thrust it in deep as she moaned in delight, her knees bending and the soles of her feet roving his arching back. He stroked the phallus into her as she writhed and made small sounds of contentment, her hands rubbing his buttocks.

The old iron bed squeaked under them; evidently the wood slats were ill-fitting, but Scott never noticed as she began to tremble and clutch him tightly, her shapely body lifting to him, her gasps in his ears—and then she moaned aloud and began to jerk under him in glorious release . . .

Her coming drew the same wild sensation from him, and he pounded into her, a frantic rush that threatened to tear the creaking bed apart and spew them out onto the floor—but it did not. They embraced, panting for breath, then kissing and moving together gently . . . finally drifting off to sleep.

In the morning, Scott Pelter received a telegram and took his leave of Jessie and Ki in the hotel dining room. Duty called him to go south at once.

She and Scott had already said their good-byes in private,

so she was able to walk out to the street with him and watch him stride away to the stables . . . without another kiss.

Ki, however, had not been lolling about. He had a plan which he wished to lay before Jessie and the sheriff.

Ebanville was the county seat, and the office of the sheriff was only a step away. Sheriff Vern Aller was an old-timer, lean and hard-eyed, a no-nonsense man who had stayed alive because he was good with a gun and never hesitated to use it. That was the gunman's edge—the will to act at once. Never hesitate. The hardcases knew it, too, and knew Aller. They stayed out of his towns. There were plenty of others.

He met Jessie and Ki in a neat, spare office that contained only a desk, four chairs, a huge map on the wall, posters of wanted men, and a rack of rifles.

"What can I do for you folks?" He ran an appreciative eye over Jessie.

"It's about the wagon train holdup, Sheriff," Ki said. "I'd like to submit an idea."

Aller squinted at him. "You a Chinaman?"

"No. Half-Japanese."

"Ummm." He looked at Jessie. "You're wearin' a gun, missy. We don't see that often."

Jessie smiled. "We have a few enemies, Sheriff. It's best to be ready."

"You know which end of that there pistol is which?"

Without a word, Jessie drew the Colt, whirled it expertly, and slid it back into the holster.

The sheriff's brows went up sharply, and he smiled. "Well, you ast a fool question and you git an answer."

"She shoots it as well," Ki said.

The older man nodded. "I believe it. Now, what was it you all had in mind?"

"A rather simple idea," Ki said. "I suggest we organize another wagon train, perhaps ten wagons—full of armed

12

men under cover. We advertise or somehow leak the information that the wagons are hauling gold, and send them out. If Reno attacks, he'll be a goner."

"A Judas train, huh?" Aller said with a grin. "D'you think it might be too obvious?"

"Why should it be? Gold—and everything else—is transported by wagons on the plains. There's no other way. This one would be just another train, except that we make sure the word gets out about what it's supposed to be carrying."

Jessie said, "It's worth a try, Sheriff."

"Yes, I 'spect so." Aller scratched his chin. "Them other wagons was sent out by Zeb Scully's Freighting Company, and it cost 'em a few dollars for cash and dead mules. I'll go talk to Zeb, see if we can organize something with teeth in it. Me and him go back forty year. You all stayin' at the hotel?"

"Yes."

"All right. I'll see you there . . ."

Sheriff Aller was as good as his word. He came into the hotel dining room the next morning as they were having breakfast. "Mind if I set down?"

"Please do, Sheriff." Ki beckoned a waiter. "Bring the sheriff some coffee."

Aller dropped his hat on an empty chair and sat, saying he had talked to Zeb and his manager and they had agreed to the plan.

"They figger eight wagons would do the trick, and Zeb will scare up some fifty riflemen to go for the ride. He wants that sombitch Reno as much as we do."

"That's wonderful!" Jessie said. "Now, how do we leak the news to the newspapers?"

Sheriff Aller grinned, crinkling his weathered face. "Zeb, he got a good idee about that. He's goin' to deny to the papers that he's hauling gold. He'll pile it on so folks will wonder. And at the same time, one of his men is gonna pretend to be mad as hell at Zeb and tell ever'one that there *is* gold on the wagon train—lots of it." Aller chuckled. "They goin' to make so much of it that ever'body in the territory will know about it."

Ki laughed. "So Reno can't fail to hear the news."

Aller said, "Hell, ever'body this side of Kansas City will hear it." The sheriff sipped the coffee the waiter brought. "Zeb will also make sure anybody watching will know when the wagons start rolling. If Reno attacks them wagons, he is gonna be laid out in Mr. Leech's undertaking parlor. With some or all of his gang—I hope."

The Ebanville weekly, the *Democrat,* came out in three days and contained a strong denial by Zeb Scully of the common gossip that he had signed a contract with an eastern firm to haul gold bullion to the Mint. He went on to say that it was nobody's business what his company hauled and that people contracting with him had a right to privacy and secrecy, and he hoped the newspapers would cease printing gossip.

Another item in the same edition mentioned the Denver Mint. In matter-of-fact sentences it said the Mint was receiving gold bullion shipments from a number of sources, hauled in by wagon trains or the railroad. The Mint's production of gold coins was up from last year's.

"A good touch," Jessie said, reading it. "Reno is bound to put two and two together."

"And fall into the trap."

The day after the *Democrat* came out, Gus Krantz, one of Zeb Scully's drivers—who had just been fired for drunkenness—got drunk, or pretended to, in the Red Star Saloon, and spilled the beans. That was a lot of cow flop, he yelled, about Zeb not hauling gold. Of course he was hauling it . . . to the railroad at Backal, to be sent to the Mint. He knew, Gus said, because he had already hauled one load.

When he had made sure everyone had heard him, Gus staggered out and into the Nugget Saloon, where he retold his story. Everyone in town knew it by morning. Gus had called Zeb a liar.

In the next issue of the *Democrat,* Zeb made a fuss over Gus's tale, denying it, and every paper in the territory picked it up to reprint—most of them with woodcuts of a wagon train.

"It's marvelous publicity," Jessie said, spreading the papers out on the bed. "When do the wagons leave?"

"In two days," Ki said. "It's about two hundred miles to Backal, and there're plenty of places for an ambush. I'm beginning to feel sorry for Reno."

"That's a mistake," she replied. "You'll be remembering his birthday next."

Chapter 3

The eight wagons were already fitted with hoops and canvas tops to shed rain and sun, and were amended so that the cloth sides could be raised in a jiffy to allow riflemen to fire in any direction. Two light trap wagons were added to the train, each with cooking facilities and supplies. There were fifty men in all, counting the wagon master.

But not counting Jessie and Ki, who joined the half dozen mounted guards.

The Zeb Scully yards were at the edge of town, but wagons headed for Backal had either to go through the town or around it to gain the trail. This one went through the town, and thus everyone saw them leave in the middle of the morning.

The wagons moved slowly, at the speed of a walking man, and the mounted men moved far out to the sides, looking for trouble. At the first sign of hostile persons, they had orders to ride back to the train at once, alerting the hidden riflemen.

• • •

They flushed no one and saw no travelers the first week. The vast plains were empty except for distant antelope and hawks; the trail was well marked. The second week, they entered a region of small grassy hills so that observation was limited and ambush guarded against. The trail wound through the hills under blue skies; the mounted men investigated each hill—and found nothing.

They had minor breakdowns—to be expected—and were sixteen days to Backal. And until they were within a few miles of the town, they saw no one.

"Reno didn't bite," Ki said. "Doesn't he want our gold?"

Jessie shrugged. "I think it's something else."

"What's that?"

"He probably has an informer in town, or two. He knows there's no gold in these wagons."

That was very possible. They discussed the matter with the wagon master and a few others, and no one had a better explanation. There were several hundred people in Ebanville, and any one of them could be in Reno's pay. It would be easy for Reno or one of his men to slip into town at night to meet with the spy.

There was nothing for the wagons to do but return to Ebanville.

Jessie and Ki left them there. They pointed across country in the direction of Korning, hoping to find the town or a road to it . . . or perhaps a pilgrim who could direct them.

It was late spring and the weather was good, getting warmer. They came across a well-traveled road the fifth day from Backal and followed it to a town alongside a shallow stream. The town was Nevers, population 304. It had five saloons and one shabby hotel.

The owner, a large-bellied man with a straw mustache and pop eyes was startled when they asked about Korning.

"What you want to go there for? Ain't no law—no nothing!"

17

"Have you been there?" Ki asked.

"Hell no! But I heard talk."

"We're looking to find somebody," Jessie explained.

"Damn poor place t'go for anything."

She insisted, "Can you tell us how to get there?"

The owner glared at Ki. "I wouldn't take a woman to that place, mister."

"Please," Jessie said. "How do we get there?"

The man sighed deeply as if terribly put upon. "The town's about two—maybe three days' ride east and a little north, in the hills . . . if it's still there. Towns has a habit of burnin' down, you know."

"Thanks."

There was a restaurant near the hotel, and they had supper there. Over coffee, Ki said, "That man may be right, of course. I mean about your going into the town."

"Shall I dress like a man?"

"I doubt if you could fool anyone."

"Even if I stuck on a false mustache?"

Ki grinned. "You'd look like a woman with a false mustache."

She lowered her voice though no one was near. "Do you think we're biting off more than we can chew, two of us against the entire town?"

He nodded slowly. "We have to expect everyone will be our enemy—if they even suspect why we're there. The first time we ask about Reno, the cat's out of the bag. We're fair game."

"That's a dismal picture." She was silent a moment, sipping coffee. "Is there anything else we can do?"

"It looks like everything's in his favor—but it may not be."

"And he may not be at Korning."

Ki sighed. "There's that."

They left at sunup and rode east, surprising deer and

rabbits on the slopes. The weather turned warmer, and during the middle of the day heat shimmers softened the horizons.

After the second day, they angled slightly north and rode far apart, keeping track of each other with binoculars.

Many times they were completely out of sight of each other for short periods. And at one of these times Ki reined in and waited for Jessie to reappear.

She was riding far east of Ki, watching for a trail or some sign of a town. The land was rolling prairie, with now and then deep ravines cutting across it.

She rode into one of the ravines to cross it—and halted, staring into the muzzles of three rifles!

One of the men said, "Where the hell you come from, missy?"

Jessie said, surprise in her voice, "I'm to meet my husband and his brother here."

Another of the men said to the others, "She's lyin'."

The first man growled. "Ain't nobody within fifty mile. What you doin' here?"

"I told you." These men were leery of her, disbelieving and on their guard. If she pulled her pistol, she might get one, even two of them but— She decided against gunplay.

She said, "I'm probably lost. I got turned around . . . We're heading for Nevers."

"You goin' in the wrong direction." They came closer, surrounding her. One snatched her revolver, and another slid the rifle from its scabbard. Then they moved back.

Jessie said in annoyance, "Are you afraid I'm a desperate criminal?"

"No, but we are," one said, and they all laughed.

They were a ragged bunch, all unshaven and dirty; they probably had been living off the land for weeks. None of them seemed to match the Reno gang descriptions.

19

They took her reins and moved up the ravine, leading her horse. One man in front and two behind.

She said, "Where are you taking me?"

The man in front looked over his shoulder. "We on our way to Korning. Nice you could come along, missy."

"What's Korning?" He did not answer.

She decided not to mention Reno Quant. It was better they knew nothing of her; let them think she knew nothing of Korning either. It might give her an edge . . .

It was obvious they had missed seeing Ki, or they would have done something about him. He would soon discover what had happened. When he did not see her in the distance, he would come looking—cautiously. So it would take time.

She glanced at the sky. She had met the three ragged men about midday. It was getting dark when they came to the town. It was a small place, not nearly as large as Ebanville, only one short street nestled up against a hill, with store buildings and a few dwellings and corrals all set down haphazardly, so the street was crooked.

It did not seem a busy place, though there were lights in most of the buildings. The three men halted, and two got down in front of a saloon. The two went inside.

One was back in ten minutes and motioned for them to take the side stairs. They climbed up to a hallway and someone said, "Put 'er in here."

Jessie went into a tiny room that smelled musty. A man told her to sit down, and she sat on the cot. They closed the door, and she looked at her new surroundings—a cot, a chair, a washbasin, and a candle. There was a window, and she got up and looked out over rooftops. She forced the window up a few inches, and better air flowed in. Did Ki know she was here in this town?

The doorknob rattled, the door opened, and a tall man entered and closed the door, leaning against it, staring at her. "What's your name?"

20

She said, "Norma Webster." She had known they would ask that question.

"And you were traveling alone out there . . . ?"

She decided to stick to the same story. "I got separated from my husband and his brother."

His lip curled. "They tell me there wasn't another soul for miles."

"They're wrong."

"You were wearing a gun and had a rifle." It was an accusation.

"My husband taught me to shoot. And we were in wild country. We were heading for Nevers."

"You were going the wrong direction." His voice held strong suspicion.

"Yes, they told me that. I was turned around."

"Do you have anything to prove who you are?"

Jessie said, "They took my warbag. I may have something in it . . ."

He nodded. "I'll look."

"Can I have it back?"

He stared at her for a moment, then nodded. "I would speculate that in the long history of this country no woman has ever traveled alone in the wilderness. What were you doing out there?"

"I told you. I was—"

He made a gesture, opened the door, and walked away. A man put his head in, closing the door. Jessie said, "Who was he?"

"Heck Jennings. He owns most of the town." He closed the door and locked it.

It was getting very dark. She found matches in a tray by the candle and struck one to light it. How could Ki find her here?

She must be a puzzle to them, and she smiled. They were probably trying to decide what to do about her. Doubtless

21

such a problem had never presented itself before. She knew there was nothing in the warbag, not even initials, that would identify her, and they were probably sure she was helpless—they had her guns.

But she had an ace in the hole they didn't know about. Ki.

★
Chapter 4

Ki waited, searching the far hills with the binocs, but Jessie did not reappear. He swore and moved toward the spot where he'd last seen her, thinking over what might have happened—she had been ambushed, or somehow fallen from the horse; maybe she'd been captured . . . He had not heard shots, but maybe he was too far away.

He stayed off the skyline and moved as fast as he dared, considering sound, stopping now and again to listen; he heard nothing out of the way.

He crossed several small ravines, but when he came to one much wider and deeper, he halted, studying it. It was about at the place he'd last seen her. He nudged the horse and went down the steep side to the sandy bottom, his hand touching his leather vest and the *shuriken* concealed there.

He had gone no more than a hundred yards when he came to the fresh hoofprints. Obviously Jessie had come down the side of the ravine and faced three horsemen. The story was plain on the sand. They had taken her north— and Ki followed, wondering if she had met Reno or some of his men. They would be very curious about finding a woman alone, and he worried that they might beat her to find out why.

Ki entered Korning on foot long after dark. The single street was nearly deserted; there were no lights along it. The only illumination came when someone opened a saloon door and lamplight streamed out.

There were several dozen horses and a few light wagons at the hitchracks and more horses and mules in corrals between the buildings. It was a very small town. Ki walked from one end to the other in a few minutes and saw no lawman's sign. A few buildings had second floors, all of them over saloons. There were probably girls in some of those rooms; they would take their "friends" there to complete their trysts.

He wondered if Jessie were locked in one of the rooms.

He prowled the town for hours but did not dare to go into one of the saloons. They were not crowded, and he would have been an object of curiosity, drawn too much attention. And in any event, he could not ask questions. That would draw more attention. How could he discover where Jessie was?

He left the town near midnight, rode away to nearby hills, and made a cold camp. In the morning, he walked back, hat pulled down, and sat on a bench in the middle of town, minding his own business. No one paid him any attention.

Then, about nine in the morning, a boy came out of a nearby restaurant and went into the largest saloon carrying a covered tray. It was obviously food. Was it for someone in the saloon—or was it for Jessie? An interesting question.

The saloon was the Three Barrels; it advertised a dance hall and a free lunch. Ki watched the boy return with an empty tray; then he got up and wandered around behind the buildings, and standing just inside a small barn, he looked over the saloon. It had a flat roof, probably tar paper, and steps rising to the second-floor door which was doubtless locked. There were four privies in a row near the lower back door, which was standing open.

Was Jessie held in that building?

Around in front again, on the same bench, Ki waited as dusk grew. The same boy came out of the restaurant with another covered tray. Ki crossed the street and said to him, "Is that for the girl?"

The boy was surprised and nodded—then he frowned and hurried on. He had probably been told to talk to no one.

Ki walked around the buildings again, smiling inwardly. She *was* in there, certainly on the second floor. Now how could he find out just where?

He had noted a coil of rope hanging on a peg in the barn. He took it down and climbed the stairs to the second-floor door. Locked, as he had expected. But it was no trick to climb to the roof, even in the growing dark. He walked silently along the edge of the roof, gazing down at the windows. Most were dark; three were not, on this side.

He crossed over. There were no windows at all on the north side.

He could hear the sounds of traffic in the street and sat down to wait. An hour passed and the sounds were gone. It was time to move.

Jessie lay on the cot as the hours dragged by. Someone brought her a covered tray in the morning—opened the door quickly, shoved the tray in, and slammed the door again. She had no chance to ask a question.

Much later a strong-looking Mexican woman came to the door and escorted her downstairs to a privy, then back again to the room. The woman only shook her head at Jessie's questions. Near dark she received another tray of food.

25

What were they going to do about her? More important, had Ki managed to find out where she was? She sighed. No one would tell him, of course. It might be an impossible task.

She closed her eyes, listening to the distant sounds of the night—and heard a kind of scratching that seemed very near. She sat up. There was a dark form outside the window! She rushed to it and pushed the window up. "Ki!"

He was holding onto a taut rope, grinning at her. "Can you climb up?"

She smiled back. "Of course."

"It's only a short distance. Hang onto the rope and don't look down . . ."

"All right . . ." She watched him walk up the side of the building and slide over the edge, as deftly as he did everything. Then she climbed out, holding fast to the rope. She managed to close the window—let them wonder how she got out—then climbed up slowly as Ki pulled from above. It took only a minute to gain the roof.

Jessie let her breath out. "How did you know I was here?"

He pulled at her arm. "Come on, let's get off this roof. Are you all right?"

"Yes, but they took everything I owned. They promised to return my things, but they didn't."

Ki looked over the edge. "Did you see or hear anything of Reno and the others?"

"No. Nothing." She followed him, climbing down to the stairs. In minutes they were on the ground behind the saloon.

In the dark street, Ki said, "They took your horse, so I suggest you pick one." He indicated the horses at the hitchracks, and Jessie nodded. She selected a good-looking bay from in front of the saloon and mounted. Ki slid up behind the saddle, and they rode slowly out of town as he told her how he'd found her.

She explained how the three men had captured her. "They thought I was alone."

"They probably had a ransom in mind. Who did they take you to?"

"A man named Heck Jennings. He owns the saloon and most of the town."

Ki said, "I've heard of him. He's wanted several places. Our friend Scott Pelter will be happy to know where he is."

They quickly arrived at Ki's cold camp. He saddled his horse, suggesting they move on at once. "Let's put distance between us and the town."

"Shall we go back to Nevers?"

"Good idea." He mounted the horse, and they hurried on.

In Nevers, they put the horses in the hotel barn. Jessie had acquired a horse with a rifle in the boot and saddlebags, which were empty. She slid the Winchester out, and they went inside and signed for rooms.

It was late in the afternoon when they arrived. There was a Ladies' Emporium across the street, and Jessie needed a few things. She went across with the saddlebags over her shoulder. In the store, she bought salves, ointments, scissors, combs, and soap, putting them into the saddlebags. And as she did that, she noticed a slip of paper she'd overlooked. It was a letter addressed "Dear Reno." It was from a town in Kansas and was from someone signing herself "Monica." She reported that Reno's Uncle Ben had died. The letter was dated two months past.

She hurried back to the hotel and showed the letter to Ki. "I think I stole Reno's horse!"

He grinned. "I think you did, too. And there's something

else." He pointed to the rifle that had been in the boot. On the stock were scratched initials: RQ. "Reno Quant, sure as a gun. Now we know he's in Korning—and probably mad as hell at losing his horse."

"And a good rifle."

"Yes." Ki frowned. "He'll hear that a woman escaped from an upstairs room—and when his horse is missing, he'll be pretty sure she took it. What will he do then?"

"Could he track us to here?"

"It's possible," Ki admitted. "And a tracker will tell him there's two of us. How far will he go for a horse?"

Reno Quant was enraged on discovering his horse had been stolen—and by a woman! "Who the hell was she?"

Heck Jennings said, "She told me her name was Norma Webster. There's nothing in her belongings with her name on it."

"How did she escape? You told me the room was locked."

"It was. And the lock is still intact." Jennings shook his head. "She must have gotten out through the window, but she couldn't have done that without help. Though how someone found out where she was is beyond me."

"Maybe one of your workers."

"Why would one of them help her? She had no money to bribe anybody. She *was* a beautiful woman—that's why I figured she'd bring a good ransom. But I've questioned my people, and they say none of them was out of sight of the others for any time at all. She definitely had outside help. Had to be."

Reno was still fuming. His horse being stolen was one thing, but his main annoyance was a boil on his neck. It was hurting more and more, a big inflamed lump that he could not touch without more pain. "Is there a doc in town?"

Jennings was sympathetic. "We don't have a proper doctor, but our undertaker, Joe Fields, had some medical training . . ."

"Get him." Reno stripped off his shirt, and when Fields hurried in, he was bent over, jaws tight, and he did not look around when Jennings introduced the man. Fields was slim and elegant, with a hook nose and long, tapering fingers. He had brought along a bottle of laudanum and suggested Reno drink some at once.

He put on spectacles and examined the offending boil without touching it. "It's a condition of the blood that causes them," he said. "The poisons are coming out," he said to Jennings. "You see how it suppurates. It needs lancing."

Reno glared around at him. "You mean cutting?"

"I mean lancing." He made a quick motion with his fingers. "Drink more of the medicine, sir. It will ease the pain. We have to get the core of it out."

"Then it'll heal?"

"Yes, it will. Drink up, sir."

Reno let his breath out and took the bottle.

Reno had put Gage Hindman to tracking the horse thief. Tracking was Gage's only claim to being worth a damn. He had been taught the art as a lad and refined it since. He was short and dark, looking much like an Indian, Nate Tupper thought, only without a feather in his black hair. He seldom had much to say, probably because nobody listened anyway when he talked. But he was a good tracker and could follow a trail where Nate could not see a print at all. But then, so could a dog.

They set out, and Vince Seeley followed along behind, content to let others lead. He was of a size with Nate and had been with Reno the shortest time.

Gage investigated both ends of town and decided the

29

south end was the most probable. A single horseman had left the town, and fresh tracks led into the sticks, where someone had hobbled a horse and made a camp without a fire. Both horses had then gone west . . .

Nate Tupper had been with Reno longest, and was truly afraid of him. Reno had an uncontrollable temper, and when something annoyed him, he would lash out at whoever happened to be within range. Nate had decided to leave him a dozen times—or shoot him when he was asleep. This was a recurring thought/wish. He could envision himself standing over a sleeping Reno and firing into his chest— three-four-five times—to make sure. Because if he did not kill him, Reno would hunt him down and tear him to bits.

On the other hand, he had put money aside—sent it to an eastern bank that Reno did not know about. One day he would slip away, when the time was right, and never return. He was sure Reno would let him go. If Reno weren't hurt, he wouldn't care.

But it would be nice to leave with Reno's share—of whatever they had to split up. Nate thought of that often, too, and of how to do it. *That* would mean Reno's death. Otherwise one day he would turn around and look into the muzzle of Reno's gun.

Gage led them to Nevers, and they entered the town late at night. They were looking for a woman and undoubtedly a male companion. It would be too unlikely she would be with another woman. They would know the woman and Reno's bay horse when they saw them.

There was one part of this that nagged at Nate. The man who had rescued the woman. Where in hell had he come from? Why hadn't they seen him at the time they'd found the woman wandering about? There was something curious about that, and not a little disturbing. Reno hadn't seemed to note it—he'd been concerned about his boil and the horse.

Nate enjoyed the idea of Reno's boil, wishing him more of them.

★

Chapter 5

In her room, Jessie and Ki discussed the situation and agreed that their next move had to be to return to Korning— at night. If Reno were still there, maybe they could figure a way to capture him. They would take advantage of any crumbs Lady Luck happened to toss in their direction.

Ki paid the hotel bill, and Jessie carried their warbags out the back. She started down the back steps to the barn— and halted suddenly, putting down the bags. One of the men who had captured her came from the barn and halted, staring at her.

She said, "You're the one called Vince!"

She heard Ki behind her, and a second man appeared in the barn door, leading the bay horse.

Then Vince went for his gun.

She was surprised, but she drew and fired and saw him stumble and fall heavily. His pistol skittered away. At the same instant, the man in the barn disappeared—as Ki rushed after him. The horse got in the way, and there was a third man, waiting in the alley on the far side of the barn. Ki saw the second man hauled up behind the other, and the horse galloped down the alley.

He went back and found Jessie bending over the downed man. She shook her head as she straightened up.

Ki said, "This one was Vince Seeley?"

"Yes. Young and foolish."

"That leaves four to go."

The town law, a deputy sheriff, knew who Vince was—one of the Reno gang. He came with others to view the body and watch the undertaker haul it away. He listened to Jessie and Ki's account of the shooting and said, "The county thanks you, miss."

When they were alone again, Jessie said, "They came after the horse."

"They came after *us*," Ki corrected. "The horse was only part of it."

"They were willing to kill someone over a horse?"

"Reno was. The gang was. Vince would have shot you—or me, except he had a bad case of the slows. But I think we'd be smart to trade the bay for another horse."

"I think so, too."

"I'll see what I can do at the livery."

Nate Tupper, with Gage up behind him, galloped the horse out of town and drew rein when they decided they were not being followed.

Gage said, "I left m'horse back there . . ."

"What happened to Vince?"

"I dunno—I got out before I got shot. There was two of them, the girl and a man."

"The man shot Vince?"

Gage nodded. "I think so. He had the drop on us. But they had Reno's bay all right. It was in the barn. They stole the horse."

Nate persisted. "But what about Vince? You didn't see what happened?"

"No I didn't—for crissakes."

"You left your horse by the stable?"

"Just inside the door. I shoulda left 'im in the alley, but I didn't figger them two to come out right then."

Nate sighed and turned the horse. They went back to the edge of town and got down in front of a land office store. As they walked to the hotel, they could see the crowd gathering with lanterns. An undertaker's wagon was just arriving.

Nate said, "They had the drop on Vince, you said? Looks like he got shot serious."

"The shot didn't come from Vince. That's all I know for sure. I ducked under the bay and got out."

"Too bad. Vince, he wasn't a bad hombre . . ."

They watched two men carry the body on a stretcher and put it in the wagon. The deceased was Vince all right, no doubts. Nate nudged Gage, and they walked back along the dark street. Reno wasn't going to like it, but it was foolish to get killed because of a horse. The man who had rescued the girl was probably a ring-tailed terror and slick as an otter to boot.

It probably wouldn't be possible to get anywhere near the hotel barn again that night. The shooting had attracted half the town; folks were still standing around jabbering. The barn might be locked up . . . Maybe no one would notice Gage's horse in the barn, and they would be able to get at the animal in the morning. Maybe.

But the stable boy noticed. He went to the owner, asking if someone had come in during the night; there was a strange hammerhead in the barn. The owner went out and looked at it, a roan with a worn saddle. He told the boy, "Go get Jack Dawes."

Dawes was the town deputy, a serious young man. He

stared at the horse and listened to the owner, then led the horse down the street to the corral beside the jail.

That night Gage Hindman stole the horse out of the corral. He and Nate rode back to Korning, agreeing on a story that sounded plausible. They told Reno that the bay horse had been impounded by the town law and they had been helpless to do anything about it.

Reno growled about the horse and swore and kicked a chair because Vince was dead. But his main attention now centered on something else, a bank in Havelock, some ninety miles to the west.

Heck Jennings had produced a man who had just come from there with a plan of the bank and copious information about same, including the fact that the law there was stupid as an army mule. The man had been alone and unable to do the job himself. It needed at least three, he thought. Jennings bought him a few drinks, and he coughed up the plan.

Jennings then asked Reno for ten percent of the take, which Reno quickly agreed to. The bank money would be cash, the total of which would never be known to Jennings. He would get ten percent of whatever Reno chose to give him.

His boil healed, Reno and the others hit the trail for Havelock.

It was daylight when Jessie and Ki came in distant sight of Korning. They found a convenient hollow to camp in, and that night Ki slipped into town hoping to learn something about Reno. But he did not. It was a chancey affair, hanging about saloons, but no one challenged him, possibly because it was an outlaw town. People were careful about asking strangers their business—or even their names.

After several nights of listening and watching, Ki thought he could be reasonably sure that Reno and his men had departed. A man like Reno ought to be making a splash in the little town, spending loot and shooting holes in the ceilings—but no one was.

"They've pulled up stakes," Ki said. "No telling where to."

Jessie suggested they return to Nevers and its modicum of civilization.

They were in time to read in the weekly, which came out the day they arrived, that the bank in Havelock had been robbed of five thousand dollars. One person had been killed. The robbers were certainly Reno Quant and his gang ... according to witnesses.

Ki said, "Damn! He got away from us." He got out a map and looked up Havelock.

It was a town on the railroad, and they headed that way at once. It was getting on toward summer, and the prairie was brown as an old hat, the sky a brassy, hard blue. They saw no one as they went across country, guided by Ki's compass, hoping they would come to a road or a trail— but they did not.

They missed the town but came to the rails, and it was anyone's guess which way the town lay, left or right. Ki flipped a coin, and they went left. Luck was with them; they found the town in less than a day's ride. It was of a more recent vintage than Nevers or Korning. Many buildings still had whitewash, and a few had been painted. The railroad had put a roundhouse there with supply sheds and workshops, and the town had grown up about them. The bank was in a red brick building, and the town law was a man who claimed to know Scott Pelter. They had been lawmen together, he said, before Scott joined the U.S. marshal's office. His name was Ford Isher, and he was older than Scott, a rather seedy individual who had been appointed to his post by the city fathers.

He told Jessie and Ki that he had already questioned the

folks at the bank and had telegraphed the sheriff with all the information because the robbers had left town and he had no jurisdiction . . . It was all he could do.

The sheriff had wired back that he should form a posse and go after the bandits, but Isher did not know where they had gone, so he had done nothing.

When Jessie and Ki called on him in his cramped office, he was visibly disturbed when he learned they intended to pursue the gang. He felt that the action would reflect badly on him. Jessie listened to him a few moments and walked out. Ki gave him a polite smile at the door and followed her.

The bank manager's name was Emmett Hibbler. He was in his fifties, gray and short, farmerish but with quick, intelligent eyes. He watched the green-eyed beauty enter the bank and come toward his office, breasts bobbing pleasantly. He licked his lips, staring at her. He had not seen a woman like that since his last trip to Kansas City— in a club his wife did not know about.

He did not notice the man behind her until she rapped on his door and gave him a dazzling smile. He invited them in. "What can I do for you?"

"I'm Jessica Starbuck," she said, "and this is my close friend, Ki. We are very interested in—"

"Starbuck!" Hibbler said. "Are you related to the late Mr. Starbuck?"

Jessie smiled. "I'm his daughter. We are very interested in running down the gang that robbed you. We are told it was Reno Quant."

"Yes, yes, yes, Miss Starbuck! We'll give you every assistance. I never knew your father, but I've heard so much about him—and I'm delighted to meet his daughter! Please sit down."

They sat in black leather chairs, and a clerk brought in coffee. Jessie said, "We talked briefly to Mr. Isher—"

"Isher is an ass!" Hibbler broke in. "Pardon me, Miss Starbuck, but he is. I don't know why the town council hired him. I've always suspected it was because he's related to one of them. He's done absolutely nothing about the robbery."

She said, "Why not start at the beginning and tell us what happened?"

"Yes, certainly." Hibbler frowned and scratched his chin. "Let's see . . . the bank was barely open that morning when the four men came in—well, three came in, one stayed just outside the door. When I saw they had guns in their hands, I was horrified! I had been robbed once before, in another town years ago, and two people had been killed when they interfered with the robbers."

Ki said, "They were waiting for you to open . . ."

"Yes, must have been. There were two customers in the bank, a man and a woman. They were put into an office and weren't harmed. Two of the robbers came over the counter, and one of my officers didn't move fast enough—and they shot him!" Hibbler paused, sighing. "They simply shot him down!"

Jessie asked, "Why do you think it was the Reno gang?"

"Because one of them called the leader—he was obviously the leader—by that name. And one of them called another Nate. We have learned since that one of the Reno gang is named Nate Tupper."

"Yes, that's true. And then what happened?"

"They just left. They were in the bank barely ten minutes, if that." He rolled his eyes. "It seemed like a year! But as soon as they killed poor Davis, they left quickly. I ran outside and watched them go east along the street—with five thousand of my money."

Ki said, "You got a very good look at them then . . ."

"Yes, oh yes, certainly." He looked hard at Jessie. "They are very desperate men, Miss Starbuck. Very."

38

She nodded. "Did you see who did the shooting?"

"I think it was Reno himself."

The other bank employees agreed with Hibbler's account of the robbery, but one had an additional bit of information they had not heard before, that was not on any of the wanted flyers.

Reno had a reddish birthmark on his neck, said a teller. He had seen the man close up. "It was on his left side."

"That may help to hang him one day," Ki said grimly.

Chapter 6

Ki unfolded the map and spread it out on the bed in his room. "Where did they go from here?" He pointed to a dot. "This is Havelock."

"Back to Korning?"

Ki chewed his lower lip. "That's a little two-bit burg, and they've got money to spend. Won't they head for some place larger, with more attractions? Korning is fine if you're on the run and want to hole up for a month."

"A larger town maybe, but they're not exactly unknowns. They're worth plenty to whoever brings them in."

Ki shrugged. "Well, as far as we know there's no tintype of any of them in existence, but good descriptions have been circulated."

"They'll use other names . . . Descriptions can be unreliable."

"So we're back to the beginning. Where did they go from Havelock? Mr. Hibbler said they rode east." He bent over the map. "There's no large town east of Havelock for a thousand miles."

Jessie tapped the map. "But there're two in the south,

40

Dakins and Marshfield. How far is the closest, two hundred miles?"

"About that, I'd say, if the map is at all accurate. That would be Dakins, population about four thousand souls." He smiled at her. "If you were a bandit, would that sound good to you?"

She smiled back. "Better than Korning."

"There's one other plus—if we go to Dakins."

"What's that?"

"There's a stage line that goes there from here. We can sell the horses and buy tickets, and sleep in way stations instead of the ground."

Jessie nodded. "That just made up my mind for me."

The distance to Dakins had never really been measured, the stage-line manager said when Jessie went to buy passage. He thought it might be about one hundred and eighty miles. He leaned forward, trying to be friendly, to get her to chat at the window so he could look down the front of her dress. But she turned away with the tickets and took a seat on a waiting-room bench.

Ki made a deal for the horses and saddles in the livery and joined her in the waiting room, to the manager's disgust. He had put a clerk at the window and had been about to ask Jessie into his office for coffee. A stream of fancy women had passed through his waiting room over the years, but damn few could compare with this green-eyed beauty. He scowled at the slim, dark man with her. A Chinaman at that! What the hell was the country coming to?

The stage arrived only a half hour late, and the hostlers hurried to change horses as the passengers saw their baggage stored and hauled themselves on board, all three of them. The third was a short citizen in a dusty brown suit who wore wire specs and had a battered carpetbag. He pulled a blanket about his narrow shoulders and went to sleep despite the jostling, bumping, rattling Concord on rutted roads.

It was a hot, dusty ride, and they were tired out when they arrived at each way station and were able to flop onto a bunk at night. The journey to Dakins took four days, including a washout that caused a detour.

Jessie and Ki put up at one of the two hotels in town, and immediately availed themselves of the hotel bathhouse—men this side, women that.

Of course there was a good chance that Reno and his gang had gone somewhere else. They might have taken the train east, for instance, to celebrate in a really big city. They might have gone to Mexico. It was the needle in the proverbial haystack all over again. They had supper and went to bed in separate rooms, both wondering if they had come all this long distance for nothing.

The next afternoon Ki came face-to-face with Nate Tupper in the Golden Rooster Saloon. He was positive it was Tupper and followed the other man to a table, where he sat down opposite a man who could have been none other than Gage Hindman. The descriptions of a dozen witnesses were accurate.

Neither of them, of course, knew him, and Ki sat watching them from the far side of the saloon. The two outlaws were relaxed and obviously unworried. They had a bottle between them and a deck of cards, which Hindman toyed with as they talked. Ki would have loved to hear that conversation, but he did not dare get too close, lest one noticed him.

After a bit, a fancy girl, who was working her way from table to table, came to them, and after some chitchat, Gage left the deck of cards and went upstairs with her. Nate then joined several others in a card game. Ki went back to the hotel.

He told Jessie about seeing Tupper and Hindman in the saloon. "I didn't see the others."

"Do you suppose they've split up?"

"Hard to say. It looks to me like they're taking it easy. Of course Reno and the young one, Sonny, may have gone somewhere else . . ."

"They've never seen you before—"

"Yes. So I can keep an eye on them."

"Shouldn't we go to the law?"

Ki sighed. "Yes, I suppose we ought to."

The sheriff's office was in a flat-faced frame building round the corner from the hotel. It had some kind of brown stain on it, which had left it streaked. Inside, the front office had a counter running the width of the building. A stout woman sat at a desk behind it, busy writing in a large, red-bound ledger. A red-on-yellow sign hung over the counter: Thomas Landon, Sheriff, Hollis County.

The woman looked up as they entered, and Jessie said, "May we talk to the sheriff, please?"

The woman got up, grunting, and went to the door of the inner office. She opened it a crack. "Some folks to see you, Sheriff."

A man's voice said, "What they want?"

"I don' know . . ." She went back to the desk.

In a moment a middle-aged man came out, taking off his glasses. He was dumpy and bald, and his weary eyes squinted at them, fastening on Jessie. They opened wider. "Yes, mum?"

"It's our duty as citizens," Jessie said, "to inform you there are several desperate, wanted men in town this moment, Sheriff."

"You don't say!" The sheriff looked skeptical. "Is this here some kind o' joke?"

"It's true," Ki said.

Landon's face became wary. "How d'you know about what you're sayin'?"

Jessie said, "We're talking about the Reno Quant gang."

43

"Reno!" The sheriff was startled. "Here in my town?"

Ki said quickly, "Well, we're not sure about Reno himself, but two of his gang are here, sitting in the Golden Rooster right this minute."

The sheriff studied him. "You the first Chinaman I seen in a coon's age."

"I'm not Chinese."

The sheriff did not seem inclined to move on their information, Jessie thought. She said gently, "There *is* a reward for any and all of them."

"Reno Quant, you say." Landon rubbed his chin. "I got flyers on them, but I got no idee what they looks like. And they's five in that gang."

"Only four now. One died recently," Ki said.

The dumpy sheriff squinted from one to the other of them. "How izzit you all knows so much about that gang? Mebbe it ain't them in the Rooster at all."

"They're there, Sheriff. I'd be happy to point them out to you."

Landon shook his head. "I got no men here. My deputies is all out doin' their jobs."

Jessie said, "You can deputize as many men as you need."

The sheriff's tone turned sharp. "Are you tellin' me my job, miss—whatever your name is?"

Jessie smiled. "Not at all, sir." She turned and walked out, with Ki at her heels.

In the street, Ki said, "He's afraid to go up against them . . . without an army."

"Yes, I suppose so."

"It's Reno we want most of all. Why don't I keep a watch on those two? Maybe they'll lead us to him."

Ki watched the two for three days, a very monotonous job. Usually starting in the early evenings, they went from

44

saloon to saloon, drinking, talking, and playing cards. They seemed to be marking time. Ki wondered if they were waiting for the other two to show up. Apparently they slept during the day, because they kept late hours.

Ki stayed out of their way, not wanting them to notice him. If there were only a few men in a saloon when they entered, he stayed outside. The sheriff and his deputies did not go near them.

Then, on the evening of the third day, Nate received a note. Ki saw a young boy deliver it, and slid out to intercept him, but the lad had run out and disappeared in the night.

Upon reading the note, Nate and Hindman cut short their usual carousing and returned to their boardinghouse at once. Ki followed, expecting them to saddle up, but they did not. After an hour passed, he realized they were not going anywhere, so he returned to the hotel and told Jessie what had occurred.

"If they're going anywhere, I think they'll ride out in the morning."

"To meet Reno."

"It's a very good guess. If it's a long ride, they would probably want to start in the morning rather than at night, wouldn't you think?"

She nodded. "So we follow . . ."

There was a stage line that ran through Dakins, and a railroad depot fifty miles north. Perhaps the two would take one or the other.

But they did not. They left the boardinghouse early, blanket rolls tied on behind their cantles, and pointed their horses' noses east. Leaving the town behind, they headed into the vast prairie without looking back.

Ki and Jessie followed all day, keeping them in sight with binoculars. At dusk, when the two got down to camp, Ki crawled close, but could not get close enough to hear talk.

In the morning, the two went on, and late in the afternoon, they separated.

"To cover more ground," Ki said. "They're looking for something."

They were looking for a cabin, and found it before dark.

Leaving his horse behind, Ki wriggled and crawled with the binocs to a ridge. Beside the shack was a pole corral with four horses. Smoke was coming from the chimney. The single window he could see was lighted.

He told Jessie, "It looks like all four of them are together."

"Did they come out here to plan another raid?"

Ki shrugged.

She persisted. "Isn't it odd that they would meet in the middle of nowhere? There must be a dozen towns they could meet in more comfortably."

"Yes, I'd think so—but here they are."

In the morning, both Jessie and Ki were on the brushy ridge with the binoculars as four men came out of the shack. Ki focused on them. "One looks like Reno." He passed the glasses to her.

"Yes, I think so." She paused. "Three are mounting up."

"Three?"

She gave him the glasses. "And riding south. They're leaving Reno behind."

"That's curious." Ki frowned. "Now he's going inside the shack . . . He's staying behind." He turned the glasses on the two who were fast disappearing. "Can you think of any reason why they would do that?"

Jessie frowned, looking after the three. "There's nothing in that direction for days."

Ki said, "Could it be a trap for us?"

"A trap?" She looked at him in surprise. "You think they

46

know we're here? That we followed them?"

"It *is* possible." He turned the binocs on the shack. "Maybe they want us to go to the shack, thinking we have Reno cornered. Maybe there're five more men inside."

"What an elaborate trap!"

He shrugged. "Spur of the moment."

"There's smoke coming from the chimney. He's fixing to stay."

Ki looked through the glasses. "He's coming out—going to the corral. Now he's leading the horse out—walking around the house to the back."

"Maybe there's a shed or something there we can't see."

"I suppose so. He's behind the shack now." He put the binocs down. "Should we move in?"

She said, "Let's wait a bit. Maybe he's meeting someone."

"Maybe the others have gone to bring him here."

She made a face. "Why would it take three to do that?"

"Ummm. Good question. But there's more smoke coming from the chimney . . ."

Jessie said, "Let's see if there're more horses behind the shack."

"Good idea." Ki led them in a long circle, keeping off the skyline, to a point where they could see the back of the shack. There was a stack of ricked-up wood and a hitchrack there—but no horse. Ki swept the entire area with the binoculars. No horse.

"He's gone!"

She said, "Could he have taken the horse inside the shack?"

"Why would he do that?"

"Let's go and see."

Ki pulled the Winchester from his boot and put it across his knees. Jessie did the same with hers, and they walked the horses slowly toward the shack.

47

They were a dozen yards from it when Ki reined in. "I don't like the feel of this—something's wrong."

She gazed at him, and he suddenly grasped her bridle, turned both horses, and they spurred away from the shack. Jessie looked back, expecting to see riflemen bursting from the house to fire at them.

But instead, the shack exploded!

Chapter 7

Bits and pieces of wood were flung into the sky. A huge dust cloud rose, boiling up, spreading out . . . There was nothing at all left of the shack.

They halted the horses, looking back. "It *was* a trap," Jessie said. "Reno expected us to go into that shack!"

"Or be close enough to be killed in the blast."

"How did they explode it?"

"Probably with a long, slow fuse—they can be timed. Reno got out of the house and rode away, keeping the shack between us and him. He lighted the fuse and lit out."

"So maybe he thinks we're dead."

Ki nodded. "We had plenty of time to enter the shack." He shaded his eyes and looked around them. "He's gone to meet up with the others."

"And where will they go now?"

Ki shrugged, gazing at the dust cloud that moved off across the prairie, dissipating slowly.

They decided to go to Marshfield. Ki estimated it to be perhaps seventy miles distant, near a stretch of badlands.

The weather turned hot as they rode; heat waves shimmered on the far horizon before them, and they made slow time. They arrived in the town in the middle of the night to see hardly a light on anywhere.

They stopped at the first hotel they came to and woke the night clerk. Ki bought a newspaper at the desk and looked at it in his room—and immediately rapped on Jessie's door.

"The gang has struck again!"

He showed her the paper. The Reno gang had robbed a bank in Bolling. Two citizens had been shot, but both would recover; the robbers had escaped. However, positive identification had been made. It was Reno Quant without doubt, including a red birthmark a teller had noted on his neck.

According to the map, Bolling was a small cow town, not on a stage line, population less than two thousand souls. The bank had lost only fifteen hundred dollars, an editor wrote. The robbers, unfortunately for them, had come on the wrong day. If they had hit the bank on Saturday, their take would have been considerably more. But since they were hightailing bandits, they could not have known that. Of course, too, on a Saturday the town would have been full of high-spirited cowhands who would probably have gone after the robbers with much gusto and filled the air with .45 slugs, so maybe the robbers were lucky after all—in a way.

Jessie put the paper down. "So where did they go from Bolling?"

Ki studied the map. It showed a spur the railroad line was building toward Bolling, but it was still a hundred miles away. The nearest town on the railroad was Denning. Ki tapped it with his finger. "That's a good possibility."

"Why is that?"

"They didn't get much from the bank. Maybe they want to try a train."

Reno was very annoyed they'd realized only fifteen hundred from the Bolling Bank. He should have known a two-bit bank in the sticks would be poor pickings. And it didn't make sense to put your life on the line for pennies. Also Nate had shot a citizen who stood in the street staring at them as if to remember every feature. Sonny had shot another who tried to block them with a wagon. That meant their price would go up.

But they were away free, with no immediate pursuit. A posse might trail them later, but Reno didn't worry about that. He had looked at the map before they'd gone into the town. There was a huge, dry lake just north of it, and they headed that way. They found it to be a shimmering expanse of chalky lake bed, hard as cement. The horses left no tracks.

Halfway across it, they bent eastward, toward the distant railroad. Reno was thinking—railroads carried treasure of all kinds. An express car might be easier and safer than a bank—with no town surrounding it to cause them trouble getting away. He had read a handful of the Billy-Be-Damned, Yaller-Backed Novels obtainable in certain stores. Their stories showed how bank and train robbers operated. The desired train was stopped by piling obstructions on the tracks—rocks or logs. Or the train was boarded while standing still, taking on water, perhaps. All that was simple enough. A six-gun would then force the expressman to open the safe, and that would be it. Much easier than going into a bank in the center of town and facing excited citizens on the way out.

When they halted that evening, Reno mentioned his thoughts concerning the railroad, and the others were all for it.

Denning was a tiny town—if indeed it could be called

a town at all. For years it had been a water stop and track maintenance depot. Now a few shacky stores had grown up around it, a saloon or two but no hotel or bank and no women. There was not a solitary female in the place, not even a wife, which Sonny Ruff very quickly discovered when they arrived.

It was his second question in a deadfall. The first was beer, the second was women. The bartender had beer.

And as he sopped it up, he got to jawing with an ex-member of the cavalry who, he said, had been mustered out at Fort Langtree a month back. His name was Pete Barnes, and he was slowly drifting eastward. He had no home and no folks, he told Sonny. He was hoping to get to a big town where he might get a job like the one he'd had in the Army.

"What was that?" Sonny asked.

"I was part of a payroll detachment. We guarded monthly payrolls."

Sonny thought that was interesting as hell, and told Reno at once. Reno and the others thereupon surrounded Barnes when he staggered from the saloon, and half carried him to a nearby empty barn, where they questioned him at great length concerning Army payrolls—which were always in cash. Each month the Army paid off in cash, greenbacks and coin, and they had never been robbed, according to Barnes.

They had no trouble getting information from the ex-soldier; he was very unhappy with the military. His company commander, he told them, had busted him back to private three times because of what he called a drinking problem, which Barnes denied. He had never been drunk on duty. Maybe a little happy, but not drunk. It was very unfair.

When Barnes began to realize the reasons for all the questions, he wanted to become part of the gang. But Reno wanted no drunks either. They let the man drift off to sleep and left him in the barn.

Jessie and Ki hit out across country, navigating by Ki's compass, and came on the steel rails the third day and followed them to Denning. It was no more than a speck on the vast prairie, a water tower with a few shacks around it.

They quickly found that Reno and his gang were not there and had not been.

"A wrong guess," Ki said, leaning on his horse. "There's nothing here. What's our next guess?"

"We decided a while ago that they'd want to spend what they had in a big town. Do we still think that way?"

"I do."

"So do I. But the trouble is, there aren't many big towns where a man like Reno could move around and not be pointed out. He's worth a thousand dollars to a bounty hunter, after all." Ki was silent a moment. "Let's think of it another way . . ."

"What other way?"

"From their point of view. They haven't been all that lucky in their last raids. Fifteen hundred, for instance, in Bolling. They haven't had much to split four ways. In a really big city, it would all be gone in a few weeks—the way they spend it."

She said, "Are you saying what I think you're saying?"

Ki nodded. "I think they'll hit another bank or two first, before they call it a season. And the nearest big town to us, with a bank, is Marshfield."

She smiled. "That's as good a guess as any."

Marshfield was a big town, one of the largest in the territory, a hub for supplies because it was on the Red Willow River, a wide, slow-moving stream that supported half a dozen stern-wheelers and many smaller craft.

It had three banks, four hotels, counting the two small five-room bunk bed houses—50¢ a night—and eleven saloons, including four hurdy-gurdy dance halls. The Merchants Hotel was the finest, and they put up there, and Ki managed to read the register. No four men together had signed in lately.

Marshfield, for all its size, was not the county seat. The local law was a marshal, appointed by the council of merchants. He had four deputies to help him keep the peace, his name was Karl Hopkins, and though he was interested in staring at Jessica, he warned them against doing any police action. "If you see this Reno Quant, you don't do nothing about it. You come t'me. Hear?"

"Of course, Marshal." Jessie smiled sweetly and went out, with Ki following.

As they left, Ki said, "It is possible he has the reward in mind."

"I wouldn't be surprised."

Ki began visiting the saloons in the evenings; it took several days to look in at all of them, and he saw no one he recognized. "They may not be in this town. What do you think of the banks?"

Jessie had visited each one, with an eye to security. "They're well protected. I'm sure Reno would think long and hard before attempting any of them."

"Then maybe that's why they're not here."

"Could they be back in Korning?"

"I doubt it. It's summer now. My hunch says they're planning something."

They entered the hotel dining room for supper. It was a pleasant place, with crisp linens on the tables, real silver laid out precisely, pictures on the walls, and even a violinist playing on the far side of the room.

Ki ordered a light wine for them, saying he did not miss

54

the long nights on the open prairie, hunched over a fire—especially in the rain.

Jessie agreed. "I suggest we stay here in town until we get some definite information concerning the gang. I'll wire Scott in the morning. Maybe he's heard something."

"Good idea."

Scott Pelter's return wire was negative. He had heard nothing they could use, he was sorry to say. He'd been busy rounding up rustlers who had raided government herds and had lost track of the Reno bunch since they had not invaded his bailiwick.

They stayed in Marshfield, and several times Jessie visited the offices of the weekly, the *Clarion*, hoping to hear something of Reno. The editor, a tall blondish man with glasses perched on the end of his nose, nearly threw himself at her feet. He bowed and simpered, holding chairs for her, shouting for an assistant to bring her coffee . . .

She suffered it all because he also went through his news files for her, laying out everything he had on the gang. He brought it to her like a puppy with his master's slippers, wagging his tail.

She took the material back to the hotel, to go through it carefully with Ki—and found an interesting paragraph: Buried in a long rambling account of Reno's deeds was a tiny item stating that Reno's mother was still alive, living in Lassiter.

"Lassiter!" Jessie said. "Where's that?"

They got the map out. Lassiter was in the upper corner of the territory, a farming area.

She said, "He might have gone there to hide out for a while."

"It's a long shot, and a long trip."

"Long shots sometimes pay off."

Ki had to admit that was true. They made preparations

to go. Ki had started down to the stable to get their horses when Jessie stopped him. The morning Concord had just pulled into town and stopped in front of the hotel. It brought a stack of newspapers from the eastern end of the territory.

The Reno Quant gang had just held up an Army payroll!

★

Chapter 8

A detachment of eight blue-clad cavalrymen guarded the light spring wagon driven by a corporal from the payroll office. Beside him sat a second lieutenant who was in charge of the detail. Two men of the group rode ahead, chattering back and forth, paying no attention to the surroundings. There had never been any trouble along the route, and the detail always followed the same rutted road coming and going.

The fort was two hours by wagon from the town and the depot, and the road wound in and around small grassy hills. The lieutenant lolled, half-asleep. It was monotonous duty, dusty as hell, and he was glad he only pulled it once every six months. Nothing had ever happened on the route, and nothing ever would.

Except that as they approached a high bluff, gunfire erupted and five of the troopers were hit and fell in the first seconds! The two mules reared and broke, spilling the wagon into the ditch, overturning it. The officer tried to rally the remaining men, but he, too, was hit, and the others scattered, having no idea how many they faced.

It was all over in moments.

Reno and the gang had thoughtfully brought sacks and quickly filled them with banded greenbacks. There were several heavy sacks of coin which they left behind because they were too bulky. They tied on the sacks and headed east. It had been one of the easiest holdups they had ever attempted. Six men were dead, but they could not concern themselves about that. They were left where they fell. None of the gang had been touched; the Army detail had gotten off only a few shots, and those into the air.

The payroll, when they counted it later, was the largest haul ever. They were rich! More than eighty thousand dollars in cash.

They counted it in a cave beside the Ramos River, some hundred miles from the anbush spot, and the three—Nate, Sonny, and Gage—demanded it be divided up at once. Reno had to agree, though he did so with bad grace. Each man received more than twenty thousand dollars. Then Gage suggested they split up for safety's sake. Anyway, it was time to celebrate. They would meet again next spring at Korning. Reno argued against it, saying there were still several months of good weather ahead of them, why waste it? But none of his arguments prevailed.

Sonny and Gage took off at once for the railroad, saying they would hit for the Big River and probably go down it to New Orleans. Nate stayed behind. He and Reno went on to Emitsville and got rooms, signing other names. And the first night, Nate locked his door and laid out all the money on the bed, gazing at it, fondling it . . . He had never had so much before, and this time he decided he would not spend it as he had before—wildly and foolishly. It would be his nest egg for the future years when he could no longer ride the owlhoot trail.

And as he put the greenbacks away, he wondered if Reno were doing the same; Reno had as much as he.

What would it take to acquire Reno's share?

He would have to kill him. There was no other way possible. Reno would have to be dead before he would give up his money. Nate shuddered, thinking about shooting the other man down. God, he'd have to be sure. Reno was a tiger and would die hard. Was it worth the risk?

Emitsville was a good-sized town, with its own weekly, and that newspaper produced an edition that played up the Army payroll robbery. It was the most heinous crime of the territory, and the Army brass declared they would never rest until the vicious perpetrators were brought to justice and hanged. Unfortunately the survivors could offer no descriptions of the ambushers. They had seen no one. The rifle fire had come from concealed marksmen—probably six or seven of them. It was a miracle anyone had escaped.

The money was bulky in the saddlebags, and they had nowhere else to put it. They could not take it to a bank. They had to keep it with them at all times. The hotel doors had flimsy locks that could not be trusted. So when they went into a restaurant, they carried the bags. In a saloon, the bags were always between their feet.

This unusual care was noticed by several who began to wonder what could be in the bags.

Despite the fact that flyers had been posted many times in towns, in stores and saloons, people did not recognize Reno and Nate, mainly because there were no pictures of them. Descriptions fit thousands. So the observant citizens who were curious about the saddlebags did not connect them to the Reno gang.

Both Reno and Nate noticed the stares, and Nate said, "You figger they know who we are?"

"Maybe not, but I think they want to look in the saddlebags. We're totin' them around everywhere."

"What else can we do?"

Reno said softly, "We can get the hell out of town."

Nate nodded.

Having too much money was always a problem. In the past, Reno had solved it by taking or sending the money to his mother in Lassiter. She put it away for him. He had a good deal of it salted away for his retirement years.

Nate solved the problem by spending it, as did Gage and Sonny.

The Army had undoubtedly hired Pinkertons to recover the payroll and corral the culprits, so Reno suggested they slide out and hightail it to Korning—and go that very night.

Nate agreed, still thinking of some method to get his hands on Reno's take. Maybe on the trail a chance would come his way. They saddled up, long after supper, when the town was settling in for the night, and walked the horses by a back street into the prairie, heading north.

However, two men saw them go. Louie Unger and Axel Fein had the hotel staked out in case of just such a move. And the fact that the two men had gone secretly in the night proved it: They had something valuable, probably money—maybe from the Army payroll—in their saddlebags. It was worth finding out.

The way to find out, Louie and Axel agreed, was to bushwhack the two. And to do that properly they had to get ahead of them and lay in wait.

But getting ahead of the two proved to be more difficult than they had expected. The two with the heavy saddlebags did not take their time; they set a fast pace and continued it, as though they had a destination and a schedule. They were also well versed in prairie travel. When they stopped, it was always in a flat area where there was little or no cover for a sniper. And they always stopped in daylight and went on at night.

Did they suspect they were followed?

• • •

They did suspect it.

As they left Emitsville behind, Reno noticed two shadows where there should have been none. His life had been spent dodging lawmen; his senses were acute and had kept him alive. Both he and Nate were wary of the unusual, and this caution was increased because of the fortunes they carried. They did not change their pace but took the road out of town—and soon left it.

Reno thought the shadows did the same. He was sure the men who followed them would not attack at night as they rode. Shooting from the back of a galloping horse at midnight was foolishness.

But they had to stop to sleep and eat. They halted in daylight in flat land and took turns sleeping and guarding. If the two shadows rushed them, Reno and Nate would have the advantage.

As he stood guard, Nate stared at the sleeping Reno. He might never have such a possibility again. But if he shot the other, their pursuers would find the body and probably close in on him from two sides. Not good. What was the point of winding up with all the money—dead?

But after the second such sleep, Reno had had enough. The pursuers had not given up. They would have to be shown the error of their ways. He and Nate were coming out of the flats into a more broken country, which was ideal for their purpose.

"We'll bushwhack 'em," Reno said. "The sombitches got no right coming after us."

Except that the two pursuers had gone around them during the last stop and were now ahead in a cozy spot, looking down their rifle barrels, waiting.

However, Reno was not a farmer. Leading the way, he did not move in a straight line in rugged country. The pursuers waited in vain for their quarry to appear, and when it was evident no one was coming their way, they had to backtrack. They had no idea where the men with the bulging saddlebags had gone. They tried to find tracks and could not. They wasted a day looking for them and finally gave up.

"Where you figger they headed?" Louie asked.

"Could be anywhere. We been snookered."

They studied the sun and did navigation in their heads, finally deciding they were closer to Levine than to Emitsville, so they started that way.

And the next day, as they approached a rocky outcropping, rifle fire spurted from the rocks, and Axel, in the lead, was knocked from the saddle, dead before he hit the weeds. Louie turned instantly and managed to get away.

The downed man was with his ancestors. His horse skittered away and began cropping grass.

Nate stood up, reloaded his Winchester, then walked to the body and turned it over. The man had fallen in thick weeds, and aside from being dead, he looked to be in very good shape. A battered leather wallet in his pocket said he was Axel Fein, with an Emitsville address. He had only a few dollars.

Reno came and looked down, "There ain't nothing we can do for him." He glanced around. "No gully to cave in over him . . . He got anything in his pants?"

"Nothing," Nate said. "Poor as a frog." He tossed the wallet into the weeds.

The man's saddle had no name on it, so they led the horse. It and the saddle would bring something in the next town.

They did not even consider going after the second man, who was probably as poor as Axel, and who was doubtless miles away by now and going strong. Let him go.

Louie Unger hurried back to Emitsville. He discovered the first time he halted to breathe the horse that a bullet hole pierced his hat, maybe an inch above his skull. He shuddered. He and poor Axel had picked the wrong hombres to fiddle with.

In town, he told the law that he and Axel had been out hunting when they'd been ambushed by persons unknown and Axel had been killed. He had been damn lucky to get away. He had no idea why anyone would try to shoot him and Axel . . . maybe for their horses?

The story caused some curiosity and was printed in the weekly.

And Jessie and Ki looked him up.

★
Chapter 9

Louie Unger did not impress either of them very much. He was living behind a barn in an added-on room. He was seedy and shifty-eyed, with too much of a whine in his voice.

"They was two or three of 'em," he told Jessie and Ki. "They jus' hauled down on us and shot poor Axel out'n the saddle without no cause or nothing."

"Two or three?"

Louie nodded quickly. It made a better story, he thought, to say there might have been three.

"And you never had a look at any of them?"

"Not a one! They never give us a holler or nothing. We wasn't expecting anything like that! Not us, out huntin' deer, peaceable. It jus' happened in a goddamn second— 'scuse me, ma'am. I dunno how I got out of there in one piece!" He showed them his hat. "Got a hole in it! Lookit that!" He poked his finger through it.

Ki said, "You were out hunting deer?"

"Sure we was. Restaurant here in town pays good for venison."

"Tell us just about where this took place."

Louie showed them on a map, and they thanked him and left. On the way back to the hotel, Jessie said, "How much of that story can we believe?"

"Not a word about hunting deer. They had no pack animal with them."

"Do you suppose they ran into the Reno gang?"

Ki frowned. "If they all met by chance out in the sticks, why would anybody shoot? People meet on roads and trails all the time. Isn't it more likely that Louie and his friend followed Reno and got hurt because of it?"

Jessie smiled. "I like that explanation better. They got too close and Reno ambushed them."

Ki agreed. "It listens a lot better than Louie's tale. He and the other one were after something—rewards maybe. Reno is wanted dead or alive."

Jessie mused, "That would put Reno in Levine about now, if he and the others are heading north."

"Lassiter is north of here," Ki observed. "And for that matter, so is Korning."

"Maybe they're going both places."

Nate Tupper had been hit. The second man, who'd managed to get away, had emptied his pistol in their general direction as he spurred off. One of the shots had sliced through Nate's shoulder, a very painful wound.

Reno bound it up, but it continued to seep blood as Nate mounted, grimacing. In the first mile, he halted and slid down, cursing his luck. Reno tore up a spare shirt to make a compress and finally got the bleeding stopped, but it hurt like blue blazes.

Reno said, "There's a doc at Levine. Grit your teeth . . . You got any whiskey?"

Nate had half a bottle and drank it down in several gulps. It seemed to help.

They continued at a walk, with Nate hunched over, drunk and hurting. It took another day-and-a-half to reach Levine. The wound was inflamed, and Nate was gray-faced when the doctor laid him on a table and adjusted his lanterns.

Dr. Packard, so his shingle said, had treated thousands of gunshot wounds, he told them, and shooed Reno out.

When he came out after nearly an hour, he said Nate would stay the night. "He's out cold," he said to Reno. "Come after him in the morning."

"How is he?"

"He'll be fine. The wound was more painful than serious."

"Can he travel?"

"I think so. I'll give him some painkiller to take along. Let him rest tonight, though."

When they reached Levine late in the evening, they took rooms in the hotel. Ki gabbed with the hotel clerk; he had not registered four men together in months. However, there had been a small convention of miners in town and he'd been busy . . . The four men might have come in two at a time, but he did not remember four men who seemed to be together.

Jessie talked to the town law. He was a dumpy, middle-aged man with specs halfway down a large nose. He had not noticed four men together who fit the descriptions.

"They a lot of folks in town, and I don't see all of 'em ever' day."

He also mentioned the miners who had whooped it up some; he was glad they'd departed and the dust had settled again. "They was wearin' out my jail."

Jessie said to Ki, "I think we've lost them. Maybe they didn't come here at all. They may have gone straight to Korning—or that other town, what was its name?"

"Landers. It's a long way west of here."

They went into the restaurant for supper. At the table, Jessie suggested they look up Landers on the map.

Ki said, "I vote we go to Lassiter first. It's a lot closer, for one thing."

She smiled. "You think a hardcase like Reno is fond of his mother?"

"No, but I wouldn't be surprised if he deposits some of his take with her for safekeeping. You recall, we had a case like that some years ago."

"Yes, that's right . . ."

Nate Tupper, standing just inside the batwing doors of the Bulldog Saloon, noticed the two who came from the hotel and walked toward the center of town. He stepped outside and followed them out of sight, then went to find Reno.

"I just seen something. We didn't git them two at the old shack."

"The Chinaman and the girl? You seen 'em here?" That was bad news. Their friend in Ebanville had warned him that the two were dangerous and tricky.

Nate nodded. "I seen a Chinaman with a girl—out on the street a minute ago. They missed gettin' blowed up."

Reno swore. "You sure it was them?"

"Course I'm sure! How many blond girls and Chinks you figger are ridin' together?"

They hurried to the boardwalk, and Nate pointed. "They went down there. They was the ones who kilt Vince. That's what Gage said."

Reno scowled. He had been sure the two had gone up with the shack. "They followed us here then. Why else would they be here?"

Nate made a face. "Hell, they figgered out what happened at the shack. They lookin' for reward money."

"I reckon . . ." Reno went into the Bulldog and sat at a

table, his back to the wall. He lighted a cigar, considering. Heck Jennings had put the girl into a locked room and she had gotten out—and stole his horse. So probably the Chinaman had helped her. There didn't seem to be any other explanation.

Then they had kept from being blown sky high at the old shack. That meant they were smart—or lucky as hell. And they were probably dangerous as teased rattlers.

But *he* was smart, too, he told himself. Smart enough not to let anger color his judgment. That was the difference between him and no-goods like Nate or the others. So give the Chinaman and the girl credit for brains, but he had brains, too. And after all, one of them was only a girl.

Nate went to the bar for beer, and Reno fiddled with a watch chain. His anger told him to go after the two and settle their beans. But judgment said: A gunfight could go either way; even an ambush might backfire. The real smart thing would be to disappear. He could go on to Lassiter and hole up there for a while, maybe even the entire winter. There was no way the two could know about Lassiter. And they'd soon get tired of poking around, finding dust.

Then, in the spring, he could go east to the Missouri and down it to Kansas City . . . and do a little celebrating on his own. There were some exciting girls in that town, and he had money. He'd told the others he'd meet them in the spring, but he might be a little late . . . depending on the girls.

Nate returned with the beers. "What you want to do about them two?"

Reno sipped the beer. "Maybe nothing."

"But they kilt Vince—and stole your horse, saddle, rifle and all!"

Reno nodded. "They sure as hell bad madicine." He squinted at Nate. "You seen folks read palms and stars and such?"

"At county fairs . . ."

"Yeah. I figger maybe them two is like that."

Nate was astounded. "You think they can read the future?"

"How else you explain why they didn't go up with the shack? They knew it was a trap."

Nate stared at him. "Dammit, Reno! Iffen that's true, then they'll know ever'thing we do!"

Reno sipped more beer. "Well, there's limits. If we can get far enough away from them . . ."

Nate gulped his beer and looked around to the saloon door as if expecting them to come through it.

Reno said, "Let's get us some vittles and slide out tonight. You go fill a gunnysack and I'll saddle the horses."

Nate finished the beer and got up.

The four men did not seem to be in Levine. They could find no trace of them. As Ki said, without a picture of the Reno gang to show, they were at a disadvantage. Descriptions were too vague.

Jessie said, "They may have bypassed the town—if they came north at all. I vote we go on to Lassiter."

Ki could only shrug. "It's as good a guess as any. Let's hope his mother still lives there."

Lassiter proved to be a small hill town; it had once been a mining camp comprising nothing but tents and shacks. Now it had real houses and a string of stores. The mines had long ago played out, but a few hundred people had remained, squatting across the north-south trail that brought travelers to the line of stores and saloons that supported them.

Ki went into the largest saloon in early afternoon and found it nearly empty. He talked to the single bartender, asking about the widow Quant.

"Quant?" The barman shook his head. "Nobody in town by that name."

"She probably lives alone . . ."

"I know ever' soul in town. Ain't nobody named Quant."

Ki sighed and went out. He reported to Jessie, "No one named Quant in town."

"She probably changed her name—married after Reno was born."

"Yes, that's very possible . . . if she's still here."

Jessie nodded. "And if the bartender was telling you the truth."

"There's that."

They asked questions of the residents: Was there an elderly lady living alone in the town? The grocer told them there were several; they traded with him. He owned the only general store in the settlement. His boy went with Ki to point out the houses. One of the women had never been married, the grocer told them. "Don't bother with her."

Another had a daughter who came to visit every month; the grocer was sure she did not have a brother. That left the third, Mrs. Haskins. She lived alone in a well-tended frame house. The grocer knew very little about her, though she had lived in the little town as long as he.

"Her name is Haskins," Jessie said. "Did Reno change his name or did she?"

Ki said, "Reno has probably changed his name a hundred times."

The boy showed Ki both houses, but Mrs. Haskins's house interested him most. The lad did not know if there was someone staying with her. He had seen no one else about the place, he said. However, he did deliver groceries to her, and she had been ordering more than usual of late.

Ki visited the house long after midnight and poked into the stable. Mrs. Haskins owned a light buggy and a mare, but there were two horses in the stalls. And a saddle hanging from a peg on one wall. It was as dark as the inside of a muskrat, and he dared not make a light to investigate further.

"One might be Reno's horse, and it might not," he told Jessie. "Shall I rap on the front door and ask them?"

"We'll have to watch the house. If Reno is there, will he stay cooped up?"

"It's hard to tell about an owlhoot."

It was necessary to watch the house from a distance, with binoculars. They saw the woman come out and tend the plants about the house, but no one else appeared. It was monotonous duty, and nothing else happened for several days. The woman occasionally went out to one of the stores and returned . . .

Ki said, "I can't believe Reno is in that house. A man like him would go crazy in four walls."

Jessie said, "See if his horse is still in the stable."

Ki slid into the stable late at night.

There was only the mare in the stalls.

Chapter 10

They left Levine behind, and several miles farther the trail branched, to the west and the north. Nate took the path westward toward Landers. His wound bothered him less and less, healing rapidly. He had tossed away the sling and had full use of his arm . . .

Reno went north to Lassiter. His plan was to join Nate in a month or so, in Landers. There was nothing to do in Lassiter, he said, but to grow older. He would leave as soon as he could.

He made sure he arrived in Lassiter long after dark, walking his horse into the little settlement when no one was around. He put his horse into his mother's stable and rapped on the house door. "It's me . . . Reno."

She got out of bed to let him in, delighted to see him. She had not expected to see him till fall.

He wanted to rest up, he told her. He had been working hard and wanted a period of peace and quiet. "Don't tell nobody I'm here."

The next day, when she went out to a store, he put most of the stolen money in the secret cement box under the house—that she did not know about. In another few years he could retire and live like a prince . . .

He had been in the house a week when his mother told him that Mr. Farmer, the grocer, had told her a strange blond woman had been asking questions. She answered the description of the blonde who traveled with the Chinaman. How in hell had she followed him here?

His talk with Nate about people who could read the future had been all joshing. Nate was an easy mark for a good story, but now Reno began to wonder. Maybe those two, the girl and the Chink, did know something. Maybe they had a crystal ball—he'd heard of them. And if they did—would he ever get a chance to bushwhack them? Wouldn't they know it—like they had known not to enter the old shack?

His best bet was to put distance between them. Distance would weaken or destroy their power.

He packed vittles and his blankets and saddled up long after dark. He walked the horse out of town on a misty, dark night, heading east into the hills. He circled the town and pointed south.

The sun's first rays found him holed up on a ridge, watching his backtrail. No one followed him.

"He's flown the coop," Ki told Jessica. "He must have gone in the middle of the night."

"Does that mean he suspects we're on his trail?"

"He might. Or maybe he's just being an owlhoot, taking no chances."

"Then we've lost him . . ."

"I'm afraid so, for the time being. We can be pretty sure he was alone here. So maybe he's gone to join the others."

"At Korning?"

Ki shrugged. "If we're still guessing, that's as good a guess as any."

They left Lassiter that same day and returned to Levine

for baths and decent beds. Ki bought the latest weekly and showed it to Jessie at breakfast. It contained an item picked up from a St. Louis paper. Gage Hindman had been accused of murder in a river town south of St. Louis, in Missouri. He had shot a gambler during a card game. Incredibly, the gambler had not been armed—when they examined the body.

Jessie said, "Doesn't that prove they've split up?"

"Yes. I wonder if it's temporary . . ."

Jessica frowned at the article. "It says nothing about whether they jailed him. He may have gotten away."

"Well, he's a long way from us." Ki sipped his coffee. "They split a big haul from the Army payroll. Isn't it likely they're busy spending it?"

"Yes . . . except for Reno, who went to Lassiter—well, we're pretty sure he went to Lassiter. He didn't spend a cent there—"

"So Korning is a good bet. Levine is closer, but he'd be recognized here."

Reno made tracks for Korning. It was a good bit out of his way for Landers, but time did not concern him greatly. Let Nate wait. He had money in his kick and there were women in Korning; he had not had a woman in much too long a time. He recalled one in the Senate Saloon named Rose or Sara, maybe Molly—one of those—who knew how to please a man. Reno licked his lips thinking about her—whoever she was. Thinking about stripping her down to bare skin as she squealed, round, red-nippled breasts rolling . . . He sighed deeply and nudged the horse.

He entered the town in early evening, put his horse in Heck Jennings's stable, and walked inside with his rifle and warbag. Heck met him, brows rising. "I didn't expect to see you so soon, Reno!"

"Put me up, Heck. I'll stay a few days."

"Yes, of course. Come this way . . ." He led Reno upstairs to a small back room. "Nobody'll bother you here."

It was a tidy room with a bunk bed, washstand, and candle in a bottle, and not much else.

Heck said, "The girls stay up in front. By the way, I got a couple new gals—"

"Yeah? That's interesting. Lemme get some sleep first."

Heck nodded and left. Reno shed his heavy coat and unbuttoned his shirt. He was pulling off his boots when someone rapped on the door. He yanked the pistol out and held it by his side. "Come in . . ."

One of Heck's bartenders opened the door. "Got a letter for you, Mr. Reno."

"A letter?" Reno was mildly surprised. He had received notes now and again, left with various bartenders by men he'd worked with, but they were few and far between. He took the letter. "Thanks . . ."

It was a handmade envelope, glued together, with no stamp. His name was on it, crudely lettered in pen. He tore it open. It was from Clay Blackburn.

"Dear Reno," it read. "If you get this before October, please meet me in Eldon. I got something you will like."

Reno propped it up on the washstand and frowned at it. October. It was still September, about the middle of the month. Eldon was a little south of Landers, not much of a burg—about like Lassiter. He wondered why Clay wanted to meet him there instead of Landers. But the last sentence was interesting: "something you will like."

That surely meant Clay had a good haul lined up. He and Clay had ridden together years ago in Missouri, wilder than catamounts, knocking over banks. Clay had wanted to stay in Missouri. He'd found a piece of fluff from a riverboat and wanted to marry her. What had happened to that? Well, so Clay was in Eldon . . .

He slept the clock round and had breakfast shortly before

noon. Heck recommended one of his new girls, Vivi. "I tried her out half a dozen times. You gonna like her."

Reno took her up to his little room. She was a pert redhead, smiling and shapely, giggling when he yanked her dress down, revealing firm, round, pink-nippled breasts— the kind he dreamed about out on the prairie. She laughed when his mouth closed over one. He laid her naked on the bunk, and she coiled her legs about him and hammered his bare buttocks with her heels as he wore himself out on her . . .

He slept late the next morning and tried out the other new girl that afternoon. She was taller than Vivi, with long, dark hair and smaller breasts, and when he mounted her, she squealed in orgasms, gasping and jerking wildly—he was sure they could hear her down in the saloon.

Heck told him later they used her in raree-shows for selected customers because she made such a screaming racket as a young stud worked between her legs.

Reno went back to Vivi.

He stayed five days, then packed his possibles and headed for Eldon. He arrived there on the twenty-fifth, five days before October.

He met Clay in the only deadfall in town.

Clay grinned, his leathery face crinkling into dozens of fine lines. "You lookin' good, Reno. Glad you got m'note." He took a bottle, and they sat at a table by the wall.

Reno said, "What you doing in these parts, Clay? Thought you liked it in Missouri."

"Still do. Still do." Clay was slightly older than Reno, lean as a rail and deeply tanned, with high cheekbones. "I figger to go back there, soon's we're finished here. Got me a place, you know."

"You're not married anymore?"

"Oh sure. Course I am. That's why I wrote you that note."

76

Reno frowned. "You ain't makin' sense, Clay. You wrote me that note because you're still married? Izzat why I come all this distance?"

"Jesus, Reno—" Clay poured out drinks and pushed one across. "Let's start over. Yeah, I'm still married, and m'wife, Mindy, is here—well, she's in Toller." He leaned over the table and lowered his voice. "She's a clerk in the bank there—usin' her maiden name a'course."

"Ahhhhh." Reno began to see the light. Toller was a town in a pretty valley across the river.

"So she hears things," Clay went on. "Maybe you read in the papers, the gover'ment is opening up some land east of here. They's already a slapped-together town on the edge of it full of lawyers and land agents."

Reno nodded. He had noticed the item and paid it no attention. Land was the last thing that interested him.

"So the bank is goin' to open a branch there come the middle of October or close to it."

Reno sipped the whiskey. "And what you got in mind?"

Clay grinned again. "Why, they shippin' money to it. They got to have cash to operate, don't they?"

"I'd figger that way. And your wife is gonna tell you when it's shipped . . ."

"Of course. Of course. That's why I wrote you." Clay's brow wrinkled. "I thought you was still ridin' with Nate and some others."

"We split up till spring. Nate is in Landers. There's time to get him. How many guns we need?"

"Prob'ly three or four, dependin' on how many guards the bank sends. Mindy says they do it in secret, startin' out at night. It's about a day's ride to the new town. I figger we could hit 'em anywheres along the way, we find a good spot."

Reno nodded. "I'll get a letter off to Nate right away. How often you talk to your wife?"

"I been goin' over to Toller twice a week. I see her about midnight in the hotel where she rents a room. She tol' 'em she's a widow woman, and her being good with figures, they hired her."

"Umm-hum," Reno said. "After we do this, she's got to stay there a spell, you know that, so they don't suspicion her."

"Yeah, I know." Clay smiled broadly. "But perty quick she'll git real sick and got to go east to a real doc."

Reno stared at him. "You done this before, ain't you?"

Clay poured into both glasses. "Yeah, we done it over in Illinois, across the river. Worked slick as bear grease, too. It wasn't quite the same, but the bank was moving money and she knew when. That was a year ago. We got enough to live high on the hog till now, with a little bit put aside. Mindy likes to squirrel it away. This here job ought to bring us more."

"Let's drink to that." They clinked glasses.

Chapter 11

The problem at Korning had not changed. They dared not enter the town openly in daylight. It was necessary to make camp outside in the woods and for Ki to slip in after dark, hoping to learn something that would be of use to them. It was a frustrating way to work.

He learned nothing at all. If Reno or any of the others were in town, they were staying out of sight—which Ki thought was not like them.

"We're spinning our wheels," he told Jessica. "Reno is five or ten steps ahead of us."

"You don't think they're here?"

"I do not."

The first light drizzle of the year helped her to suggest they return to Levine. Reno could be anywhere—and so could the gang.

Reno was in fact only about sixty miles south, in Eldon, waiting for Clay to return from a visit with his wife in Toller. Clay expected she would have the date of the money transfer.

But she did not. The date had not yet been set, she told Clay. "But I am sure it will be within the next ten days. They're boxing up a lot of things to take along. And they're also painting a sign."

Clay rented a room in the same hotel, telling the clerk he was passing through on his way south. He slipped into his wife's room when no one was around and went out before anyone was up in the morning.

He would return in three days.

Nate Tupper showed up in Eldon, having received Reno's letter. He had enjoyed himself in Landers, he told Reno. There were some eager girls in the hurdy-gurdy house, not too expensive and very willing.

He said, "What we fixin' to do?"

"We're goin' to hold up some messengers who are delivering money to a branch bank," Reno said.

"How much money?"

"In the neighborhood of fifty thousand," Clay replied.

"That's a hell of a good neighborhood."

There was very little to do in Eldon but play cards, eat and drink, and dream about how to spend a large amount of money. Clay had decided to take Mindy west to San Francisco, he said. He had heard about the Pacific Ocean but had never seen it. "Maybe it ain't there . . ."

Nate was considering traveling to New Orleans to join Sonny and Gage. Reno thought privately that he would first return to Lassiter with his share, to put most of it in the cement box under the house. Then he might spend some time in Korning with Vivi—maybe hire her for a week at a time. A man could pack a lot of diverting into a week. What was the point of riding all that way to New Orleans for the same thing?

● ● ●

Clay's wife had the date when he returned in three days. It rained when he rode there, but it was a small storm and quickly passed on toward the east. He returned from Toller all grins.

He said, "We can leave here in two days and find ourselves a good bushwhack location. Mindy says she thinks they will be a wagon, a driver, and four guards. That's the usual. The wagon is painted with bright blue trim, with the bank's name on the sides."

Reno rubbed his hands together. This was going to be as easy as the Army payroll had been.

There was a well-defined road from Toller to the new town at the edge of the land to be opened. It was rutted from hundreds of horses and wagons and wound through hills and rolling prairie. They noted several excellent spots, but Reno turned them all down until they came up on one that pleased him, the one that would put the bank travelers at the most disadvantage. The road made a sharp turn to round an outcropping of pale granite rocks that thrust up a dozen or more feet like jagged teeth. The rocks provided a hundred niches and crannies for rifles. The bank wagon would pass within fifty feet. They couldn't miss, Clay said.

Reno gathered some small rocks and piled them in a pyramid at the side of the road. "When the wagon reaches the rocks, everyone fires at once. If the horses stampede, we shoot 'em down. All right?"

They agreed.

Then they waited.

A day passed slowly. Several seedy pilgrims came along the road from the new town, obviously not interested in land. Toward noon of the second day, they saw dust in the distance.

"Somebody coming," Nate said, shading his eyes. In a few minutes he added, "It's a wagon and some riders."

"Get ready," Reno warned.

"Look for the blue trim on the wagon," Clay said. "No sense shootin' the mail."

Reno curled up behind the rocks, hugging his Winchester to his shoulder, finger caressing the trigger. It was the right wagon; he could see the blue trim easily. He pulled the hammer back and moved the front sight to center on the leading rider, a man in a faded denim jacket and a battered brown hat. He had a rifle across his thighs—and barely a minute to live.

Reno could hear the clatter of iron-rimmed wagon wheels on hard ground, the patter of hooves, and even the squeak of leather—then the wagon reached the little pyramid of rocks. Reno squeezed the trigger. A fusillade of shots swept the driver off the seat and the riders out of their saddles. The team reared and started to run. Reno fired at the near horse, and it went down heavily. The wagon smashed into it, heaved up on its side, and turned over. Someone shot the other horse, and suddenly everything was still; the firing stopped.

Nate said loudly, "That's all of 'em."

Reno got up, walked around the outcropping to the road, and frowned at the wagon. All four wheels were in the air, one slowly turning. Boxes and papers were strewn everywhere; a light breeze picked up some of them and scattered them into the weeds. Evidently the bank had sent along printed forms and other papers as well as the money.

He kicked the wagon. "Let's turn this thing over . . ."

They righted the light wagon with one heave. The money was in a heavy iron-strapped box with a padlock. They struggled it out of the wagon bed, and Clay drew his revolver and shot the lock off.

Inside, greenbacks were packed in neat paper wrappers. Nate stood over it. "Ain't that a perty sight!"

It was indeed. They bundled the money up in several

sacks and rode back to Eldon, arriving well after dark. Clay had a small frame house on the edge of the little burg, and they gathered there to divide up the pie.

They dumped it out on a table, and Clay and Reno sat down to count it with Nate watching, licking his lips to see so much green, wondering how he could get his hands on more than just his share . . . The total take was exactly forty thousand dollars.

Clay was slightly disappointed. Mindy had thought there would be more. Each of them received a bit more than thirteen thousand; not as much as the Army payroll, but considerable.

Reno said, "Maybe they figgering to send more another time."

Clay grunted, stacking his pile and squaring the edges. "If they do, they going to send along a damn cavalry patrol to guard it." He sighed deeply. "We had our chance and this is it. Now all we got to do is dodge the Pinkertons. They going to be all over the landscape like bluebottle flies."

Reno growled. "We didn't leave our names back there . . ."

"Well, me, I'm pointin' for Missouri."

Nate said, "You ain't goin' to wait for your wife?"

"We can't be seen together," Clay replied. "She'll get pretend sick in a couple weeks and git on a stage. I'll meet her in Kansas City, and we'll head south to my place." He grinned at them. "Maybe we'll pull this here game next year."

The public outcry over the multiple deaths of the bank messengers—the newspapers were calling it a massacre— caused Reno and Nate to remain in Eldon for the time being, along with Clay, who decided not to travel with so much cash until the hue and cry had died down. "Give it a few weeks," he said.

He rode to Toller and visited his wife in secret. She would put off her "sickness" for a while. She and all the bank employees had been questioned, and everyone was aghast at the murders. The Pinkertons were into everything, she told Clay. "How much did we get?"

At the same time, Nate rode back to Landers to take up with a girl there. He hid his pile and took along only a small amount of money, in case he happened to be intercepted. When he returned to Eldon, he had an envelope with Reno's name on it. It was from their friend in Ebanville, an unsigned warning. Korning was about to be invaded by a force of Pinkertons and other lawmen! Stay away!

Reno had decided to go to Korning, his mind on Vivi, but the warning undecided him. There was nothing to do in little Eldon, and he fretted . . .

Clay's several weeks lengthened into three. He visited his wife again, and they arranged a meeting time and place in Kansas City. Clay assumed a disguise to wear on the stagecoach. He bought a Bible and dressed as a minister; the same disguise had served him well in the past, he said.

When he left, Nate insisted that Landers was the place for them, and he had no opposition from Reno. They saddled up and left at once.

★

Chapter 12

Landers was about the size of Korning and was situated on the edge of a long, crumpled area of badlands. This made it handy for certain citizens to duck into in case of need. However, Landers was a town without law—and without much plan. It had a single main street that was generally straight, with but few doglegs. The several side streets were hardly more than paths. Shacks and tents decorated the areas behind the stores and saloons, and chickens pecked in the grass.

The local undertaker was perhaps the busiest man in town. There were shootings every night. The bodies were hauled out to the boardwalk to await his wagon each morning. He was paid whatever happened to be in the pockets of the deceased—including his watch, if he had one. And his pistol.

These items were displayed for sale in the undertaker's window, at reduced prices.

Nate and Reno took rooms in a boardinghouse but spent most of their time in one or another of the dozen saloons. Reno enjoyed a certain celebrity; he was known to all. His posters were displayed in quite a different spirit from how they were displayed in other towns. Men bought him drinks and vied to sit at his table, playing cards with him.

He and Nate toted their bulging saddlebags everywhere, and no one doubted what was in them. Details of the bank-messenger massacre were known to all.

In Landers, both men took to wearing two pistols, one on the hip, one under the arm. When he sat at a table, Reno put his back to a wall and laid one revolver on the table in front of him. Reno was notorious for his hair-trigger temper, a man who shot first and inquired about the deceased afterward.

But he knew a great many hardcases, and one of them was Carter Sanderson. Years in the past, in Missouri and along the river, he and Carter had held up any number of pilgrims, relieving them of whatever. Carter, who called himself by various other names, was now in cattle, he told Reno.

He had found it easy and profitable to move small herds from one range to another. He sold the cows to smallholders who did not worry overmuch about such legalities as bills of sale. "A cow looks like a cow, don't it?"

Carter was a rangy, weathered, soft-spoken sort who did not look in the least like the thief he actually was.

"Stealin' cows is much safer than stealin' from folks who might shoot back," he said. It was the kind of logic the James boys understood.

Nate also agreed, rubbing his recent wound. But Reno was not interested in that life. It required a man to spend far too much of his time under the stars, rain or shine or dust. He preferred a few weeks of intensive planning, then hit the job, whatever it was, and skedaddle with the booty.

But everyone to his own druthers. Carter was a pleasant companion, and they soaked up considerable whiskey, jawing. Carter was between herds and would probably lie up till spring, he said

Reno also went upstairs frequently with one of the girls he had taken a fancy to, Maud, who reminded him of Vivi. He would spend an hour or often two, with his boots off, lolling with Maud, who had everything off.

Nate noted these visits and thought about them.

There was no stageline into Landers, but travelers brought newspapers, all of which mentioned the big raid at Korning. A number of wanted men had been rounded up and were in various jails awaiting justice. But, the papers said, the notorious outlaw, Reno Quant, was not among them.

A few newcomers in Landers, who had happened to be in Korning when the law invaded in force, and who had slid out before the net descended, said the law had stayed in the town for three days, then left with the prisoners in wagons. Korning was gradually recovering. Heck Jennings was not wanted by the law and had not been bothered, but there was gossip that the same tactic would be used on Landers. No one knew when, of course.

The weather turned bad; rain and wind buffeted the town, and the main street became a quagmire. For a week people huddled by the fires and stoves, then the rain slackened and let up and the sun came out. During the week, Reno spent much time with Maud, stripped to his long johns in her warm bed. He enjoyed the way she babied him, fed him and soothed him. In her bed, he could forget the rest of the world. How pleasant it was . . .

Then, on one of those occasions when Reno went upstairs with Maud, Nate followed them after five or ten minutes. The upstairs consisted of two parts: living quarters for the owner and a section for the girls—five tiny rooms at the top of the stairs. All the rooms had flimsy doors, no locks.

Each had only a simple bit of wood that turned on a nail to hold the door closed.

At the back of the building was a door leading to the steps down to the alley. The door was usually locked on the inside with a bolt.

There was a single lantern at the head of the stairs, providing a dim light. When Nate went up, three of the girls' doors were standing open, the rooms unoccupied at the moment. He could hear the murmur of voices from one of the closed doors. He listened at Maud's door, hearing only the bed squeaking.

Returning to the saloon, he gave it his full attention, thinking about the money in Reno's saddlebags. That money had been on his mind constantly; every time he saw the saddlebags, he grit his teeth. He owed Reno nothing; he had no qualms about stealing it . . . if that were possible.

He thought about the situation. The upstairs rooms were tiny, containing only a bed each and some clothes pegs on the wall. There was not even a chair. A simple washstand was at the far end, away from the door; there was very little space for the saddlebags. They were probably on the floor just inside the door. If he opened the door silently, the bags ought to be within easy reach. And Reno ought to be so occupied he would hear nothing. He might even be asleep.

Would he ever get a better chance?

The next day, when he and Reno were together, Nate began talking about Texas and San Antonio. He was thinking, he said, about going down along the border.

"A damn long trip," Reno said.

Nate agreed and let it hang. He didn't want to be too obvious, just plant the seed.

He let three days go by. Then, late in the afternoon, when Reno went upstairs with Maud, Nate brought his horse from the hotel stable, only a few doors away, to the alley behind the saloon. His warbag was packed, the blanket roll tied on; he was ready.

He went upstairs. Two of the girls were busy with customers; there was laughter and muted conversation. He heard whispers from behind Maud's door, then silence. He waited for what seemed a long time. Did he hear heavy breathing? With his knife, he eased the wooden pin up and opened the door silently. He was on his knees, his head lower than the bed. The couple in the bed seemed to be asleep.

The saddlebags were on the floor in front of him. He snaked them out without a sound and closed the door.

His heart hammering, he sneaked to the back door, unbolted it, ran down the back steps, and flung himself on his horse. If Reno caught him now, he was a dead man!

But it would probably be another hour at least till Reno discovered his loss. He had that much of a head start. He pointed the horse's head west, out of town. Reno would think he'd gone south to the border, wouldn't he? First Reno would have to discover that he, Nate, was gone. Reno would have no idea who had stolen the saddlebags. It might have been anyone. It would take him another hour to realize the truth. Nate grinned in the gathering dark. He had the money! His own and Reno's! Thousands of dollars! He would go to California and change his name, even grow a beard. He might buy a small ranch in some out-of-the-way spot. Reno would never find him. How could he? He could not investigate every person in the entire United States!

He'd have to make up a good story, too, where he came from and all, but that should be easy.

But maybe California wasn't far enough. He could go down into Mexico and live the rest of his life on what he had in the saddlebags. He pictured himself sitting on a veranda with a servant to bring him drinks and cigars as he gazed over his acres. Could he stand that, as a permanent thing? No more riding hell for leather in the night, no more shooting up a town; no more excitement! Just sitting there, getting a little older each day . . .

Nate sighed deeply, pulling his coat tighter about him. It was cold, and he had no idea where in hell he was bound. He turned to look back. Nothing but gloom. But from now on he would be looking over his shoulder . . .

He went on through the night without stopping. The sky was dark and overcast, and he rode through a light mist, followed by a drizzle that stayed with him for hours. But it did not rain. He was on the high plains, heading into the wind. Maybe he ought to bend north and catch the railroad that climbed over the Rockies, all the way to the coast. Riding in a comfortable car would beat horseback any day, and be a lot faster. He was eager to put as many miles between himself and Reno as possible.

By morning Reno would certainly have discovered that his money was missing and that he, Nate, was also gone up the flue. He'd put those two facts together in a hurry.

And Nate could imagine Reno's fury!

★

Chapter 13

Jessica and Ki did not go along on the raid into Korning, but they arrived there the day after, bearing a telegram from Scott Pelter that vouched for them. When he read the wire, the deputy U.S. marshal received them politely. "What can I tell you?"

"We're interested in hearing about Reno Quant," Jessie said.

"So am I." The marshal smiled. "Unfortunately we didn't find him in the rounded-up people. None of his gang were here either."

"We were hoping . . ."

The marshal shrugged. "We had information that he *was* here, but hard to tell how long ago. It's almost impossible to get the truth from the people we bagged. I'm sure they'll lie to St. Peter if they ever get to the Pearly Gates—which I doubt."

"Thanks, Marshal . . ."

They stayed in the town till the wagons left with the prisoners, more than fifty hardcases, who were still astonished that the law had come to Korning in that manner.

But there was nothing in the town to interest them—since Reno was not there—and they returned to Levine. As Ki said, they were still too many steps behind the outlaws.

The bank-messenger massacre was headlined in all the papers because of its viciousness. Not one had survived, and forty thousand dollars had disappeared. There were no clues. The Pinkerton chief on the job declared that he was confident of an arrest soon.

"This thing was like the Reno gang," Ki said. "It's the way they operate. It's a copy of the Army payroll holdup and shooting."

"Except that we know the gang is not together. If Reno planned this one, he recruited others to help."

They were in the hotel restaurant, and Ki scratched his chin. "The thing that bothers me is, how did they know the bank would be sending money at that precise time?"

"You think there was an informer?"

He nodded. "How else would they know? They were obviously waiting for the delivery. It could not have been hit or miss."

"Let's go talk to the bank manager."

Ki smiled. "I was about to suggest that very thing."

The bank in Toller was owned and managed by Geoffrey Lane, a tall man who was beginning to spread out in middle age. He was nervous and obviously under much strain when they were shown into his office. The loss of forty thousand dollars was a terrible blow because it would come out of his pocket.

"I did everything possible to insure the delivery was safe," he told them. "It was sent in secret—"

"How many knew about it?" Jessie asked.

"Only a very few. As few as possible." He almost wrung his hands. "I assure you—"

"Exactly how many?" Ki asked.

"Myself and my chief teller. No one else."

"How did you arrange it?" Jessie asked.

Lane took a long breath. I went to Marshal Ingram—he's our town law, you know—and told him I needed five or six men for a delivery. Preferably men who were honest and who could guard a valuable shipment. I did not tell him exactly what the shipment was, nor did he ask. But he provided the men and I hired them. They all seemed like—"

"You knew none of them personally?"

"No, I did not. They were told they would be guarding a shipment of bank records. Nothing was said about money."

Ki said, "So many men to guard bank records?"

Lane shrugged slightly. "I explained to them that the records were very valuable to me. At any rate, they came to the bank at night, loaded the wagon, and departed."

"And were ambushed," Ki said. "Somebody knew about the delivery. How many work in the bank?"

"Six, not counting myself. But I assure you, none of them—the Pinkertons have already questioned them at length, you know."

Jessie said, "May we talk to your chief teller?"

"Of course . . . certainly." Lane led them into the next office and introduced them. The teller, Lawrence Haley, was thin and almost wispy. He wore thick glasses and constantly adjusted them. Lane left them with him.

He told them essentially the same story that Lane had, and insisted that no outsider could have known about the delivery. He fussed with the glasses and steepled his fingers, assuring them that all the bank employees were loyal and honest. All of them had been with the bank for years, except one, a woman bookkeeper who was single and above suspicion.

"Who is she?" Ki asked.

"Her name is Mindy Sharpe."

Jessie said, "Is it possible she knew about the shipment in advance?"

"The Pinkertons asked me that same question." Haley fussed with papers on his desk. "I . . . I don't see how—"

"But it *is* possible?"

The teller sighed. "Yes—I suppose it's possible . . . I suppose it's likely that everyone in the bank's employ knew something was afoot. But Mindy is certainly above suspicion! How could she be in cahoots with criminals? How could she know men who would kill like that?"

He pointed the clerk out to them—a slim, soberly dressed woman who looked to be about thirty-five, busy at work, seated at a desk piled with papers. Jessie had to admit to herself that Mindy Sharpe did not look like the kind of person who would run with killers.

Was it possible she was the weak link?

Ki thought it possible and did not want to question Miss Sharpe for that reason. He said, "If she has any connection to Reno or one of his gang, she won't stay here long."

Jessie agreed. "But what if she has no connection to them?"

"Then we've wasted some time is all. Let's look into her past, as much as we can."

She was their best bet, Ki thought, mostly because she'd been with the bank the shortest time, much less than a year. She had suddenly appeared and asked for work, and had proved to be an excellent accountant. She had a letter of recommendation from a bank in Missouri.

Jessie and Ki read the Pinkerton reports. According to them, Mindy and the other employees checked out. The Pinkerton report had been done quickly, and Ki thought Miss Mindy Sharpe's past seemed hazy. The chief teller, Mr. Haley, confessed with some embarrassment that he had not contacted the Missouri bank to confirm her letter, taking it on face value because she was obviously well qualified.

But she was a model of decorum. She was a single woman and lived in the Toller Hotel and was never seen with men. She spent her free time alone and seemed to have no interest in anything but her job.

Jessie and Ki took turns observing her, following her movements, but she never contacted anyone and kept regular hours. And she never received mail.

"She's too good to be true," Ki said disgustedly. "I'm afraid we're marking time again. Let's try something else."

"You know there's another theory—"

"What theory?"

Jessie smiled. "What if the owner, Mr. Lane, is behind it? Robbed his own bank."

Ki laughed. "Why in the world?"

"Maybe the bank is failing and he is about to abscond with the forty thousand."

Ki shook his head. "The Pinkerton report says the bank is in very good condition. I think that report is accurate."

Jessie sighed. "There goes an interesting theory."

"We're at a dead end."

The Pinkerton organization was thorough and had reported that there was no leak in the bank itself. The information received by the robber/murderers had to have come from some outside source. Maybe from the branch site, where the money was being sent. The Pinkertons were swarming all over that area, questioning everyone.

After ten days, Jessie and Ki returned to Levine. Winter was upon them, and they suspected the Reno gang was holed up somewhere to wait out the storms. Sooner or later Reno would surface . . . probably when he needed money.

Ki visited the saloons in Levine, listening, hoping against hope for some scrap.

But nothing.

• • •

Then he met Hetty.

She was young, maybe twenty-five, and worked in a millinery shop on the main street. She was accosted at dusk by two half-drunk peelers as she was walking home to her boardinghouse. They mistook her for a soiled dove and were mauling her on a side street when Ki came along.

He told them to let the girl alone, and they swore at him, threatening him with broken bones. It was their second mistake. Ki flipped one onto his back, where he lay moaning. He hurled the other into a brick wall, caught him, piled him on his companion, and let them both moan.

Then he escorted the girl home, learning her name—Hetty Thompson. She was astonished. "How did you do that so easily?"

"Long practice," Ki said. "Did you know either of them?"

"No! Certainly not!" She grinned at him. "But I doubt if they'll bother me again."

"Perhaps I should make sure of that . . ."

She said quickly, "I usually leave the shop at five."

She wore no wedding ring, he noticed, and lived alone. Her father was dead, and her mother lived in Nevers, not too far away. She worked in the millinery shop because she was part owner.

At the boardinghouse, she thanked him for his opportune help and he left her, humming to himself.

The next day Jessie received a letter from Mr. Lane at the Toller Bank. Mindy Sharpe had become sick and after a few days had taken the stagecoach east—exactly as Ki had predicted she would do—if she were guilty. Lane wrote that she had gone east to find a more qualified doctor to treat her illness.

Ki read the letter. "So she was the leak! She got a job

with the bank and took advantage of inside information. In this case, a shipment of cash."

"Let's hope the Pinkertons are after her."

Ki was at the shop the next day at five, and Hetty did not seem surprised to see him. It had been raining but had let up, and they walked to her boardinghouse in the still, cold air, chatting of nothing in particular. They stood on the porch for a while, then Hetty went in and Ki hurried back to the hotel.

The third day was much the same, except that a dance was to be held in the Methodist church on Saturday evening, and Ki asked Hetty to come with him. She accepted eagerly.

At the same time, in New Orleans, Sonny Ruff shot a salesman who had punched him in the face in a foolish argument over a stool in a saloon. The salesman happened to be unarmed, and took several minutes to die.

In the excitement, Gage got Sonny out and hurried him away in the dark before the police could arrive.

Unfortunately for Sonny, the deceased had a brother on the force, and a number of friends who were incensed at the murder. Sonny was badly wanted—every officer in the city was looking for him. A very good description was printed and distributed everywhere.

He and Gage stayed out of sight in a transients' hotel for nearly a week, with Gage bringing in food, while the hue and cry was in full swing. When the newspapers said the police were of the opinion the murderer had escaped, Gage made a deal with a fisherman and they were taken across the river at night in a smelly boat. From there, they bought passage on a small stern-wheeler bound upstream.

There were only a half dozen passengers aboard, and on the third day, Sonny became aware of the steady gaze of one of the boat's crew. He mentioned it to Gage, and they decided to leave the boat in secret. They found a chance at night, at a wooding station. When the boat went on, they trudged inland and bought horses at a farm, then set out west across southern Missouri, pointing for Korning.

Sonny had always been clean-shaven, but now he let his mustache grow, and it changed his face completely. He did not much care for the effect, but Gage said it was a marvelous disguise. "Your own mother wouldn't know you!"

They were more than a month on the journey, pushing through storms and detouring around flooded areas, but when they arrived, they found Reno there.

He seemed glad to see them, and neither mentioned the dead salesman in New Orleans. Gage wanted to know, "Where's Nate?"

Reno was still in a rage about it. "The sombitch stole my money!"

"Where'd he go?"

"If I knew, for Crissakes, I'd have gone after him a long time ago. He talked about San Antone, but that's a damn far piece. He ever talk about any hideout to you all?"

He had not. Neither had had any idea Nate was capable of such a terrible thing. He had never given them an inkling. Gage asked, "How'd he do it?"

Reno told them, and they shook their heads. Nate had taken one hell of a chance.

Their money was mostly gone, both admitted. They'd had one whale of a time in New Orleans, scattering money as if it were barley seed. Several girls were much richer than they had been, not to mention saloon keepers.

Reno was also low on funds; he had only what was in his pockets when Nate had filched the saddlebags. Privately he thought of returning to Lassiter, and only the thought of snowdrifts decided him to wait. Heck Jennings agreed to advance him money . . .

He had no plans for the spring. Something would turn up. "Come grass, we'll think about it," he told them.

★

Chapter 14

The Saturday night dance was held in the church's largest room, with most of the chairs removed. A single row was put along three walls for spectators, and tables at the end of the room contained glasses and a large bowl of pink punch that had no spirits in it. Some of the ladies had made small cakes and tarts.

A very sedate crowd showed up in Sunday clothes. The three musicians were those who played for the regular services—piano, violin, and guitar.

It had snowed that night and morning, but the stars were out, and it was very cold when Ki called for Hetty. She appeared wearing a heavy coat with a scarf about her head, and took his arm; they walked to the church in the middle of the road, avoiding the icy patches.

She wore a blue dress with tiny white ruffles and a pert little bustle. He hung her coat on a peg and nodded to the others as they found chairs. The musicians were playing and everyone was talking at once. Hetty seemed to know all the women; they had all been in her store at one time or another. Ki brought her some punch, and a few brave souls began to dance in a very serious way.

The punch tasted vaguely of lemons but was very bland. A man dying of thirst would gulp it down, Ki thought, but not if he could get plain water.

The musicians were playing tunes he had never heard before, and he wondered if one of the three had composed them. They all sounded somewhat alike, and each had a slow tempo. The evening had a rather funereal air, Ki thought, and he began to feel sorry he had brought Hetty. They ventured onto the dance floor once, but when the number was finished, they hurried off.

Behind her hand, Hetty whispered, "I keep wondering if someone has died and we're at the service."

"It's not permitted to smile," Ki whispered back.

She giggled. "The punch is terrible."

"Oh," Ki said, "it isn't *that* good." He leaned close. "Why don't we slip away and have coffee in the restaurant?"

She nodded quickly. "Good idea."

He collected her coat and helped her on with it in the vestibule. She tied on the scarf and approached the front door. Two heavyset men were there, and one of them said loudly, "I didn't know they allowed Chinks in here."

The other laughed. Ki looked at them; they were standing in the doorway, glaring at him. He said politely, "May we pass, please?"

"Why, certain sure," one of them said. They stepped aside and allowed Hetty to go out, but closed in again, smiling at Ki, showing big square teeth. Ki smiled at them, gesturing. "Would you gentlemen like to step outside?"

Looking mildly surprised, they quickly stepped through the door, and Ki closed it behind them. The two turned on Ki, their faces taut and harsh in the mealy light. They were about to show this Chinaman he wasn't wanted here. As they reached for him, Ki kicked out, and one swore and bent double. Ki chopped down on the man's exposed neck then

101

pushed him into the other. Jumping in close, Ki elbowed a pistol away and chopped the second man alongside the head, and he went down atop his companion. It was over in seconds.

Taking Hetty's arm, Ki walked away as if nothing had happened.

She said, "You're a wonder! Those were two of the town toughs!"

"I'll apologize to them next time we meet."

She laughed. "I think if they see you again, they'll run away!"

They had coffee in the almost deserted restaurant, sitting at a table. She was full of curiosity about him. "You're not Chinese . . ."

"No, half-Japanese." He told her he'd been on his way to San Francisco when a wagon train had been held up by the Reno gang. He had stayed to help capture the bandits.

"Then you're a lawman?"

"No, just an amateur—with some experience in those matters."

She smiled. "You don't look very dangerous, but you certainly took care of those men! And I notice you don't wear a gun."

He turned the conversation to her. She had been in school, hoping to become a teacher, when her father died. He had left her some money, which she had invested in the millinery shop, and it provided her a living. The major owner of the shop was an elderly woman, Mrs. Wade Tully, a widow, who talked of selling out to Hetty one day when the shop got to be too much for her.

"She's getting on and wants to retire with her grandchildren around her," Hetty said. "That's why I stay. But when the shop's mine, I will probably sell out, too, and open a shop in Nevers, closer to my mother."

102

Ki walked her home and this time gave her a peck on the cheek.

Nate Tupper was lucky enough to see rooflines in the distance as the snowstorm swept down on him, pelting him with white. He got to the town as the heavy winds hit, bringing thick snow swirling everywhere, a full-blown blizzard. He put his horse in the livery and hurried across the street to a shacky hotel with the saddlebags over his shoulder. The owner was glad to see him; his rooms, all five of them, were empty of guests. "Take any one you want."

Nate took the first he came to, shoved off his boots, pulled the blankets over him, and slept the clock round.

He was ravenous when he woke late the next day. The snow was two feet thick outside and still coming down. There was only one restaurant in town, the owner said.

"What is this place?"

"Fenton," the other said. It had been named after the oldest resident, long gone to his Maker. The population was probably less than two hundred souls. Fenton had once been a mining town, but no longer. The copper veins had played out, a familiar story. The town was dying. Half the buildings on the main street were boarded up. Fenton had nothing to offer but loneliness.

"Me, I expect to pull up stakes come spring," the hotel owner said. "So does half the town. We'll git back to civilization."

The restaurant food was not all that good, so Nate went into the general store and bought bread, cheese, and airtights and then took them back to the hotel. It looked very much like he was going to be snowed in for a while.

The storm continued for several days, gaining in strength, and the snow piled high. It was the worst storm in this section of the country, the hotelman said, at least in his memory. It was impossible to travel, and impossible for Nate to tell how long he would have to wait before going on.

He could not leave, but on the other hand, Reno could not reach him. For the time being, the storms were his friend.

Seth McKann, weathered, tired out, and pushing fifty, drifted into Korning on the heels of a departing storm. He had a few drinks with Heck Jennings; they were old friends but had not seen each other for going on twelve years. Seth was sure of it, because he had spent the last five in prison, with plenty of time to review every one of the days . . . and dream about what might have been.

He had been drifting since he'd gotten out, afraid to return to his old line of work—armed robbery. If they caught him at it again, he'd stay inside till they rang down the curtain.

"Prison's no good," he said to Heck, and shuddered. "I don' want no more of it."

"Yeah, five years is a long time."

"Too goddamn long. Makes a man feel old and useless when he gets out." Seth grinned weakly. "I guess m'nerves is shot to hell. Just thinking about goin' back gives me the willies." He sighed. "And I know a good thing, too."

"A good thing? What's that?"

Seth smiled and lowered his voice from force of habit. "They's a store in Benders just askin' for it."

"A store?" Heck made a face.

"Wait a minute." Seth reached across the table and grabbed the other's wrist. "They got their own safe—figger it's as good as a bank's. It's a big store, biggest in the territory they say—do a hell of a business. Come the end of the week, that safe is bulgin'."

Heck nodded. "You looked it over good? What you going to do about it?"

"I'm not goin' back inside!"

"Can you draw a plan of this place?"

"Sure I can."

"How about if I know some gents who would be innerested? You figger the plan and take ten percent."

Seth nodded quickly. "Long's I can stay right here. Who you got in mind?"

"Reno Quant."

"Reno! He still alive?"

"He's right upstairs this minute. Finish your drink. Let's go up and talk to him."

It was not the hardest winter they had ever experienced in Levine, the old-timers said. Six years ago, they all agreed, they'd had a doozie. However, the snow piled high between the stores and houses. It was shoveled off the walks by volunteers, and business continued . . .

Old Mrs. Tully, the widow woman who owned the greater share of the millinery shop, lived in the small quarters built on behind it. She had only to open the rear door and she was home.

Hetty had to walk the several blocks to her boardinghouse, bundled up, and she could have no male visitors in her room; it was not fitting for a young woman to entertain men without others present.

Ki frequently walked with her from the shop to the boardinghouse, chatted with her on the veranda for a time, then went back to his hotel. He could think of better arrangements. But none seemed possible in Levine.

Jessie sometimes spent time near the hotel desk because there were newspapers and periodicals to be had. And one afternoon she was introduced to a woman who had recently lost her husband to sickness. She was Mrs. Roy Wiley, and Jessie was delighted—though she did not show it—to learn the woman's husband had owned and run a saloon in

Korning. Upon her husband's death, Mrs. Wiley had sold the saloon to her brother because she knew nothing about such work. When Jessie's brows rose in mild surprise at the saloon's location, the woman said, "All the merchants in Korning are not thieves, Miss Starbuck."

Her husband, she told Jessie, had inherited the saloon from his father when the town was respectable. The shady elements had come in gradually and had finally taken over the town. However, the older merchants were not all that much affected. People needed the goods and services and paid for them, and only occasionally did the hardcases cause trouble. Then then men like Heck Jennings stepped in and settled whatever problem had arisen.

She knew men like Reno Quant, Mrs. Wiley said, and disliked them, as did a good many others. Reno had caused her husband needless trouble and expense, and she wished him ill. "He ought to be behind bars for the rest of his life!"

When Jessie confided that she and Ki were set on bringing Reno to justice, Mrs. Wiley wanted to help. "Is there anything I can do?"

Ki told her the difficulty he'd had in entering the town and learning anything about Reno. She offered to write to her brother, asking him to help Ki in secret.

"But don't get my brother in trouble!"

Ki promised.

★

Chapter 15

"It's the biggest store I ever seen," Seth McKann said. "Course I ain't been to Kansas City . . . But I got friendly with a clerk—sombitch sopped it up, and he told me the owner never used a bank. Has his own safe. He doesn't trust banks 'cause he was helt up one time."

"How much you figger is in the safe?" Reno asked.

Seth shrugged. "No way to know. Maybe he empties it now 'n' then. Puts it some'ere's else. I seen the safe, though, and it's a big jasper. I got a fast look at it—it got its own room—when somebody opened and closed the door quick. Maybe it's got ever' dollar the store ever made in it. And maybe not. No way to know."

"Just one owner?" Heck asked.

"Far's I know."

"Where's he live?"

"Across the street from the store, in a hotel. His wife went east a few years ago and never come back." Seth grinned. "Lots of talk about that. They say she ran off with somebody."

107

"He lives in a hotel?" Reno said. "Then it ain't likely he got another safe. You think?"

Gage said, "Hotels got safes, too."

"They got little ones, yeah," Reno said. "The store got a big one in its own room? Is they a back door to this store?"

"O'course, a big wide one. Big enough for a wagon to back up to it. But I got a idea . . ."

"Draw us a plan." Reno provided a pencil. "Floor plan with the back door. How many stories to this building?"

"Two stories, that's why I got a idea."

Heck said, "The store take up the entire ground floor?"

"Yeah, and it's all locked up good. They's iron bars on the front when it's closed, and the back door's got heavy irons across it, like a goddamn fort."

Reno frowned at him. "I thought you said this was a possible thing? Now all of a sudden it's a damn fort! Can we get in a window?"

"I don't think so. The side windows is all small and high up, and the street windows is barred, too, at night."

Reno sat back in disgust. "What the hell, you brought us nothing."

Seth smiled at him. "You want to hear my idea or not?"

"What idea?"

"The store's on the ground floor. Upstairs is offices, some dentists and others. I looked it all over real good. I figger a hole could be cut in the floor to get into the store—"

Gage yelled, "Yeah! A hole in the goddamn floor!"

"—on Sunday when the store's closed."

Heck asked, "Anybody on the second floor on Sunday?"

"Nobody I seen. Closed up tight," Seth said. "But no iron bars. There's one door to go through, but a crowbar can fix that. I figger they never thought of somebody goin' through the floor."

Reno smiled, a rare occurrence. "You jus' made ten percent."

Gage looked out the window. "Le's wait till it stops snowin' for crissakes."

"Won't be long," Seth said.

"This store's in Benders? What's the law in that town?"

Seth said, "They got a new marshal, an old-timer. He got three deputies." Seth shook his head. "You all go into the upstairs after dark on Saturday night, and you won't see hide ner hair of them. Then you got all Sunday to bust the safe and get away. They won't discover it till Monday morning."

"I vote we do 'er," Sonny said.

Gage nodded. "Me, too. Sounds like shootin' fish in a barrel."

Reno frowned. "What about noise?"

"You all make a hole in the middle of the building. They's walls all around. Who's gonna hear?"

Ki rode alone to Korning, bearing the letter from Mrs. Wiley to her brother. It was too dangerous for Jessie to accompany him. It was foolish to take chances; she did not like to see him go alone, but Ki was not helpless . . .

The letter was addressed to Enoch Cobb at the Cougar Saloon, and asked Enoch to give Ki every assistance without betraying himself.

Ki gave him the letter at closing time, when the saloon had emptied out. Cobb read it quickly, and locked and barred the front door. He led Ki into the back rooms, his living quarters. "Where's your horse?"

"In front," Ki said.

"Bring 'im around back to the stable."

Ki nodded and went out. When he returned, Cobb demanded, "What you want in Korning?"

"Reno Quant," Ki said simply.

109

"Jesus!" Cobb was startled. "How you figger to do that?"

"I don't know. Is he in town now?"

The other nodded. "He hangs out in Jennings's place. They're old friends, 'cording to the talk. I never had any truck with Jennings . . ." He found a cigar and looked at it critically. "What you want me t'do?"

Ki smiled. "I need a place to stay—"

"That's easy."

"I can't go down to Jennings's saloon, but I need to listen to people talk. There's an outside chance I might hear something I can use."

Cobb nodded vigorously. "There's one hell of a lot of talk goes on in this saloon." He squinted at Ki. "Lookit here—" He led Ki around into a storeroom behind the bar. It was piled with boxes and sacks. He went to the wall and opened a slot. "Look through that."

Ki put his eye to the six-inch slot; he could see the entire saloon.

Cobb said, "The first owner of this here place had trouble with bartenders stealin' from him. This's how he caught 'em. You think it might help?"

Ki nodded. "It sure might."

Cobb had a spare cot and blankets, and Ki bedded down.

The next day, when the saloon opened for business, Ki listened at the slot. He could hear everything that was said by men at the long bar.

But nothing they said was of any interest to him.

Reno decided they would wait until the weather allowed easy travel. None of them had any desire to buck the snowdrifts and put up with freezing rain. "That store," he said, "ain't going nowhere."

Being very low in funds, Seth was unhappy at the decision, and Reno had nothing to give him. So he went from store to store and made a few dollars shoveling snow—

and drank it up quickly. It did not take much to get him drunk, and he tended to run off at the mouth when he was. It was a condition Reno did not know about.

Seth had shoveled snow for Enoch Cobb and was drinking in the saloon when he mentioned the store job, how they were going to cut a hole in the floor. He was happy with the idea, a hole in the floor, repeating it over and over again, swilling beer and laughing.

Ki listened idly. He had been hearing plans for the spring, rustling and robbery . . . the kind of thing men talked about in Korning.

And then the man mentioned Reno. He said the name only once, but Ki heard it.

Ki got a good look at him and was outside the saloon when Seth came staggering out. Ki led him to a barn that was empty and encouraged him to gossip. It took an hour to get the story. Reno was planning to rob a store in Benders by cutting a hole in the floor of an upstairs office.

But the drunk did not know when the robbery would take place. Reno would go when the snows let up. Ki could get nothing else out of him. He left the drunk in the barn.

Enoch knew the man's name—Seth McKann.

"Is it true?" Ki asked. "That he knows Reno?"

Cobb was certain he did. "He knew him in Missouri years ago."

It did not storm every day, and when the weather cleared and a weak but willing sun came out, slightly warming the land and curtailing the icy winds, Ki rode back to Levine.

In Jessie's hotel room, he told her what he had learned.

She said, "What's your opinion? Is it good information?"

"I think so. He was drunk as sin, but the idea of cutting a hole in the floor rings true. It's not the kind of thing a drunk would invent."

"But you don't know when it's to take place."

Ki shook his head. "It's not long till spring."

Jessie suggested they go to Benders and look the store over. If Reno was planning to rob it, it must be a big one, and maybe the only big store in town.

Ki agreed and they prepared to go at once.

He walked home with Hetty that day and she seemed glad to see him, but he sensed that their situation had changed. And it had. She'd had a chance to think about it, she told him. She did not want to become involved with someone who would probably be away much of the time, despite the attraction she had for him . . . Did he understand?

He understood completely. And he could not blame her for it.

In early spring, Reno, Gage, and Sonny rode to Benders. They entered the town one at a time, hours apart. Reno was last, long after dark. The town had two hotels—a merchant's hotel and a six-bit house. He stayed in the better one and let Sonny and Gage put up in the fleabag.

Then Reno, dressed as an ordinary citizen, went into and looked over the largest store, Johnson's Mercantile. Seth was right, it was a big place; a large brick building with offices on the second floor. The stairs were around on a side street behind a stout door that stood open during the day. Reno went upstairs, to find several dentists, a lawyer, a land office, and a photographic studio. Two offices stood vacant.

There were four roads out of Benders. Reno decided they would go south and west and cut across country for Marshfield, a large town. They ought to be able to lose themselves in it till the furor died down.

As Seth suggested, they would go into the building late on Saturday night. Gage bought tools—an auger, a saw, and a crowbar. Sonny bought a length of rope. All were concealed in the hotel stable.

• • •

Jessie and Ki arrived in Benders on a blustery day and went at once to the Johnson store and asked to talk to the owner, Kit Johnson.

He saw them in a large, square office. In it were a huge rolltop desk and shelves laden with files, papers, and books; there were framed documents on the walls, a turkey carpet on the floor, and several padded chairs.

Johnson was a big, untidy man with wrinkled clothes, wire glasses, and a salt-and-pepper beard. He looked appreciatively at Jessie and asked them to sit and state their business.

Jessie said, "We've come to offer what help we can—"

"Help?" Johnson said in surprise. "I need help with what?"

Ki said gently, "You're about to be robbed."

The store owner stared from one to the other of them. "Robbed! What d'you mean, robbed?"

Jessie explained, and Johnson stared up at the ceiling. "They're coming through from the upper floor?"

"That's the plan."

"But you don't know when?"

"Unfortunately, no. Maybe even Reno doesn't know that. But we're sure it'll be soon, now that the weather is turning."

Johnson stared at them, fingering his beard. It was a moment before he spoke. "If they get in here, the way you say, they'll have one hell of a time getting out. There's bars and chains on the doors and windows with padlocks . . ."

"They will probably go back the way they came. They doubtless figure to have plenty of time," Ki said.

"What about your safe?" Jessie asked. "Can they get into it?"

Johnson fiddled with papers on his desk. "It's supposed to be burglarproof—we never had anybody try to bust into

113

it. If they use dynamite, they'll blow everything inside it and wreck half the building. Is this Reno any good with explosives?"

Jessie shook her blond head. "We doubt it."

Johnson hired five men who were vouched for by the local law. Two of them were off-duty deputies. They were placed in the store each night to watch for intruders. They were instructed to close in and arrest anyone who came into the store after hours, especially anyone sliding down a rope from the second floor.

A week went by and nothing happened.

★

Chapter 16

Two of the offices over the mercantile store were vacant. Either of them would be fine for the hole they would make. Late on Saturday evening, Gage and Sonny pried the downstairs door open with the crowbar and, when Reno entered, closed it again carefully.

They lighted a lantern in the vacant office, and Sonny went to work with the auger, boring a hole in the floor. When the hole was large enough, they inserted the saw and finally opened a rectangular hole between the floor beams. With this done, they tackled the ceiling boards the same way. These were punched through and dropped clattering to the floor below.

They had knotted the rope every fifteen inches to make climbing easier. They tied it to some water pipes and dropped it down. Then Sonny slid through the hole and started down the rope in the darkness. He had matches to light a lantern when he reached the floor.

Halfway down he heard sounds and stopped, peering around. There should have been no one in the store. Was that someone moving? Did he hear a metallic click? There were guards in the store! He began clawing his way up, yelling to them to pull him up.

Someone fired from the darkness, then a fusillade of shots—and Sonny dropped. He was dead before he hit the floor.

Instantly Reno ran for the stairs, with Gage close behind. They ran down to the street door with pistols in hand—but no one had thought to station men there. They flung themselves on their horses and spurred away into the dark.

The five men hired by Kit Johnson had been on guard inside the store for too many monotonous nights in the pitch dark. There was nothing to do but sit and wait. They had no idea where the hole in the ceiling would be made, and when they finally heard the augers and the saw, their nerves tightened. After all, it was Reno Quant, the killer, up there.

When one of the robbers finally came through the hole and began to climb down, they were all on edge, fingering guns, jaws tight. And when the man stopped and shouted, trying to get back up, the tension broke and one of them fired. Then they all fired.

But the other thieves got away.

Jessie and Ki remained at the hotel; there was nothing they could do in the store to help the guards.

They did not find out what had happened until the next morning, when they went to the store and were surprised to see a crowd there. The undertaker's wagon was also in front of the store, with two men loading the body of Sonny Ruff. Jessie identified it quickly for the undertaker. "He was one of the Reno gang, the youngest."

"Are you certain?"

"Yes, absolutely. I saw him close up many times."

The undertaker did not ask how that had happened.

One of the deputy guards explained what had occurred in the store. Sonny Ruff had been climbing down the rope, then trying to get back up when somebody fired. The guard did not know who. "But then ever'body opened up," he said. "That gent is fulla holes."

"But Reno got away," Jessie said in annoyance. The man who had gotten buck fever had wrecked the entire operation.

However, Kit Johnson was pleased. He had suffered only a hole in his ceiling, which would quickly be repaired. It was no skin off his butt that the big fish had gotten away. He was well pleased and thanked Jessie and Ki profusely.

Ki remarked when they went back to the hotel, "When all's said and done, we're whittling them down. Only three of the gang remain."

"Yes, but we should have had them all." Jessie was still annoyed. It was the kind of opportunity that would probably never come again.

Nate Tupper was one of the few strangers in the little burg, the only guest in the hotel, and the only one who carried his saddlebags everywhere.

He stayed in the hotel most times, sitting by the big belly stove, feet up on the ring, two revolvers in plain sight. A number of people noticed the saddlebags—and the guns. And no one doubted that the stranger had something of value in the bags. Probably money.

And a number of people wanted it. But the stranger had a competent look to him. His pistol grips were well worn. He studied everyone who came near him; he was probably a gunslick. No one wanted to find out.

The stranger was in town because of the weather. Travel was hazardous on roads that were quagmires when it rained and impassable with chest-high drifts when it snowed. And with roads buried in snow, it was easy to get lost. That could be fatal. The prairie was a sea of white, and there were no road signs.

It was obvious that the stranger was waiting for better weather.

And three young men—Lew Pitts, Jason Krug, and Coby Drain—met in Lew's house and talked about the saddlebags. How did one separate bulging saddlebags from a gunman who did not want to give them up?

Wouldn't it have to be done by a ruse of some sort?

But what? All three were young and agile, and handy with guns, but none was a gunslick. Very few men were. The stranger sat by the stove, but could not be shot from outside because the single window was impossible to see through.

They discussed shooting him when he came out to go to the general store, which he did now and then, but it was impossible to know when. It would mean one of them would have to stand out in the freezing weather to wait. None was keen about that. And anyway, if they shot him in the street, everyone would know about it and who had done it. There was a county sheriff to worry about.

However, the weather decided them; it turned warm. A bright sun melted the snow and even partially dried the earth, enough to make travel possible. Nate Tupper packed his possibles and set out, riding to the north, where he expected to catch the train west.

Lew Pitts saw him go and ran to corral the others. "He's gone—heading north!"

They piled on their horses and chased after the stranger. He was five miles or more north of the town when he noticed them. Pausing on a hillock and glancing back, he was surprised to see three horsemen galloping after him.

And he knew instantly what they were after.

They were possibly a mile behind him on flat ground when he first glimpsed the movement. Quickly he tied the horse behind the hillock, yanked out his Winchester, and saw it was loaded. Then he crawled to the ridge and found a good spot between craggy rocks to lie full-length with the rifle thrust out before him.

He was certain they hadn't spotted him, because they came on full-tilt until they were a short distance away. Then they slowed, seeing the rocks, but still came on, warily, walking the horses in single file.

What they wanted was on his horse, poor fools, Nate thought. They had maybe one chance in a million of getting it. The man in the lead had no chance at all.

Nate drew back the hammer and settled the butt of the rifle into his shoulder. He put the front sight on the leading rider and waited. He'd let them come to within about sixty yards . . .

He took up the trigger slack and held his breath as he squeezed. When the rifle fired, the leading man slumped, his rifle fell, and he hit the ground hard and lay still. The horse reared, and the other two men broke right and left instantly. Faster than Nate had anticipated. Maybe they'd had training in the war. He fired at one—three-four-five times—aiming at the horse, but did not stop him. Damn! Then both were out of range.

Nate pulled back and reloaded automatically. He remained where he was for a time, the Winchester ready, but he did not expect them to return for a fight. They'd had enough— surely they knew their companion was dead.

After a dozen minutes, Nate climbed on the horse and went on.

Lew Pitts was dead as a rock. The stranger had hit him in the ticker with one shot. They made sure the man was long gone before they ventured close to the body and turned it over. Poor Lew . . .

Jason said, "We got to make up a good story about this. Can we say it was a hunting accident?"

"That's as good as any."

They hung the body over Lew's horse and went back to town, walking slowly.

Nate went less than three miles before he halted, looking at the sky. The three men had chased him for the money he carried. No doubt about it.

He swung about and stared at his backtrail and slapped the saddlebags. How many more would get ideas like that?

What he had to do was change the shape—put the money into something that looked more ordinary, like a carpetbag. God knew, half the country carried carpetbags. They were cheap and efficient and took a lot of battering even if they were ugly. He should have thought of it sooner.

He nudged the horse and went on. Maybe he could buy a bag where he caught the train. Or if it came to that, he'd steal one.

Jessie was surprised and delighted when Scott Pelter showed up in Levine one afternoon. She had just come to the door of the hotel when she saw him get down and tie his horse at the hitchrack.

She hurried down the steps. "Scott!"

He turned with a smile and took both her hands. "Jessie! You're even more beautiful than the girl I've been dreaming about! How do you manage it?"

"You've been dreaming about strange girls?"

He laughed. "Oh, it's so good to see you!"

"What're you doing here?"

"We wrapped up some cases—and I wasn't far. I took a chance you'd be here." He pretended alarm. "You've not met someone and married him?"

"No, of course not." She laughed and took his arm. "Come, buy me a cup of coffee . . ."

"Where's Ki?"

"He's somewhere around." They went into the mostly

120

deserted restaurant and sat at a corner table where they could see the street.

He asked, "Are you still chasing Reno Quant?"

"Yes, but not with much success."

"I heard about the attempted robbery at Johnson's Mercantile. It came over the wire next morning. So they killed one of the gang . . ." He shook his head. "They should have gotten all of them."

"It was botched," she said. "You should have been in charge."

He smiled. A young man with an apron over his jeans took their orders and went away. Scott said, "Well, there'll be other times, I suppose, if you keep after him. Do you intend to?"

"Yes, certainly. The trouble is finding him. He's very elusive. How many days off do you have?"

He sighed. "Only three. I have to be in Ebanville on the fourth day. There's been more and more cattle rustling in the south. My boss, the marshal, wants to stamp it out."

"Only three . . ."

"For him that's generous."

The coffee came, and the boy in jeans departed.

She said, "We were very disappointed that the marshals didn't catch Reno in the Korning raid. Are you going to do that again?"

He shrugged. "I have no idea. That's up to the big brass. But, as you know, it's hard to second-guess criminals. They seldom do what you want them to do. You're staying in the hotel?"

"Yes." She smiled and pressed his hand. "The second floor, room six."

★

Chapter 17

Nate Tupper reached the railroad three days after leaving Fenton. He followed the rails west for two more days and came on Tyler—a water tower, a line of sheds, half a dozen stores, two saloons, and some corrals. He felt very good. It was a bright day, not too cold, and there was no hint of a storm in the sky.

He slid down in front of the general store and stretched. Three or four men were sitting in the sun near the livery, one of them whittling, a very peaceful scene. Nate went inside the store, and a little bell rang. A wizened old man with an apron about his middle was sitting by a stove smoking a pipe and reading a newspaper. He lifted his glasses and nodded to Nate. "Howdy." He got up and walked to the counter stiffly. "Nice day t'day . . ."

"Yep," Nate said, looking at the shelves. "When's the westbound due?"

"Westbound train?" The old man blinked. "Tomorra, I think. Yeah, tomorra, Wednesday."

"It stops here?"

"Allus does, yep. Got to take on water."

The door opened and the little bell clanged. Nate saw the old man's eyes widen, and he looked around—and looked into the muzzle of a .45.

A lean, white-mustached man said, "Put yore hands on the counter."

Nate said, "What the hell!"

The older man yanked back the hammer. "You heard what I said."

Nate growled, but he put his hands, palms down, on the counter. "What the goddamn is this?"

The storekeeper said, "Howdy, Deputy, who's this here?"

The deputy snaked out Nate's pistol and shoved it in his belt. "I figger him for one of the Reno gang."

Nate looked over his shoulder. "Me—the Reno gang! Jesus, you out'n your mind! You got the wrong man."

"The hell I have. You answer the description perfect."

The deputy deftly tied Nate's hands behind him and sat him down by the door.

Nate said, "You makin' a big mistake, Deputy. Maybe I look like somebody, but I ain't one of the Reno gang."

The lawman shrugged. "I takin' you to Calvin. If you ain't—we let you go. How's that?"

Nate groaned.

The deputy put him on the eastbound train, and they rode half a day to the county seat, Calvin. It was a town about the size of Levine but with a large courthouse and jail. Nate was put into one of the cells and told to shut up.

Another deputy was dispatched to Havelock to bring back a witness who could identify Nate—or not. When Nate was told about it, he did shut up.

His goose was cooked when that man arrived.

Scott Pelter came to Jessie's door that night and tapped on it lightly. She let him in and bolted the door; the room was dim. She had blown out the lamp, and a single candle was glowing on a washstand across the room from the bed.

She slid into his arms. "It's been such a long time . . ."

He said, "You refuse to stay in one place very long."

"I can't deny that." She laughed, sat on the edge of the bed, and patted it. "Come and sit here with me. We must get reacquainted."

He sat and took her hand, kissing it. She pulled it away and moved closer, snuggling into his arms again, kissing him hungrily. Then, after several long minutes, she tugged at his shirt, and he slid it over his head and tossed it to a chair.

"Now your boots," she said, and helped him tug them off. As he slipped off his jeans, she unfastened her dress. He lay back on the bed, naked, and watched her as she delicately removed the last shred of dress and bared her ripe, round breasts.

Smiling, she jumped onto the bed; he was erect and eager for her. This was like old times in Ebanville. She gathered up the pink shaft in both hands, kissing it as he stiffened and sucked in his breath. Then she slid onto him, scissoring his body, guiding the shaft—it entered her deeply as he writhed. His hands caressed her velvety skin, and he pulled her down for a long kiss.

Then he rolled her over, and her legs tightened about him. The bed rocked under them as he thrust and stroked into her as she moaned softly, arms holding him in a drowning grip. She was moving sinuously, sighing, rubbing her bare feet on the backs of his legs. He gasped, driving himself wildly, to the very edge—and then over it—mingling his moans with hers, shuddering in release . . . as she kissed him softly.

And then for an hour or more they continued, driving themselves to climax over and over again till at last they tapered off and slept in each other's arms . . . And the candle snuffed itself out toward dawn.

• • •

When a reporter heard that a suspected member of the Reno Quant gang was in the Calvin jail, he immediately interviewed the sheriff and wrote a story which was printed locally and reprinted by every paper in the territory and as far distant as Kansas City. KILLER APPREHENDED!

Reno Quant was news. And depending on the trial, his henchman might be in for a hanging. Nate read that in jail and shuddered.

In due course a copy of one of the papers came to Korning and was read by Heck Jennings, who took it to Reno.

"You wanted to know where Nate is? Well, he's in Calvin, waiting trial."

Reno grabbed the paper and read it quickly. "Damn! They got him—so they got the money, too!"

"They confiscated it."

"That stupid Nate Tupper! Got himself taken in a little one-horse burg! It says here a deputy recognized him from a description. And they got a witness coming from the Havelock Bank to identify him." Reno let out his breath. "Damn him!"

Heck frowned at the paper. "You think they can make Nate talk before they hang him?"

"Prob'ly . . ."

"They might make a deal with him to get you."

Reno scowled. "How could they do that?"

"I dunno. But I bet you they try. I guess it depends on how much Nate knows about you."

Reno instantly thought of Lassiter and the money he had stashed there. How much did Nate know about that? Probably quite a bit. He wouldn't know exactly where the money was hidden, but he could probably be sure it was somewhere in the house. A determined search would surely turn up the cement box—and then he'd be flat. Every penny gone. The damned law would take it all. And for squealing, they might give Nate a long prison term instead of the rope.

The more Reno thought about it, the more it worried him. Nate was sure to tell them about the money at Lassiter. He had proved he was a son of a bitch, hadn't he? Of course he would tell them.

Reno had better get there first and find another hiding place for it!

And this was a job he had to do by himself. He couldn't send anyone else. There wasn't anyone in the world he trusted enough.

He went to the nearest window and looked at the sky. It was clear, not a cloud in sight. He made up his mind in a moment. He had to go to Lassiter—now! With any luck he'd get there before another storm hit.

Heck Jennings was astonished when he said he was leaving. "Where the hell you going?"

"Something I gotta do."

"But Nate is in jail! You can't get at him!"

He let Heck think he was going after Nate. "I gotta be sure."

"They'll see you hanging around. Let the law have him!"

"Stop yammerin' at me." Reno rolled his blankets and pulled on his gloves. He left town at sunrise of a cloudless morning, heading west toward Calvin, but turning north out of sight of the town. How fast would the law move? It probably depended on how fast they beat it out of Nate.

The spate of good weather had melted much of the snow, and Reno made good time. It was cold as hell, but he could endure cold. He could not endure the loss of all that money.

She hated to see Scott go. But his duty called. She rode with him, a mile or so out of town, so no one would see them kissing good-bye.

Ki was in the hotel reading a newspaper when Jessie returned. He showed her an item. Nate Tupper had been arrested and was being held in the Calvin jail on murder charges. Emmett Hibbler, from the Havelock Bank, had gone to Calvin and identified Tupper as one of the men who had robbed him of five thousand dollars and killed one of his clerks.

The trial would be held soon, and it was a foregone conclusion, the paper stated, that Tupper would be found guilty. After Hibbler's testimony, he was a goner.

The paper was a week old, and maybe the trial was already history, Ki said. "And maybe Nate is too."

"If so," Jessie said, "there's only two of them left, Hindman and Reno." She folded the paper. "What's your guess, are they in Korning? We know that Reno goes back there frequently."

Ki nodded. "I wouldn't bet against it." He scratched his chin. "I could go back to Enoch Cobb's place for a few days. We might get a line on them that way."

"It could be dangerous . . ."

"Or boring," he said.

Paunchy Emmett Hibbler stood in front of Nate Tupper's cell and stared at the man inside. "That's him. That's the man they called Nate."

"I am not!" Nate yelled. "My name's George Wilson! I never seen this man before in my life!"

Hibbler shook his head. "He's a robber and a liar."

The sheriff asked, "Is he the one who shot your clerk?"

"No, that was Reno himself."

"I don't know no Reno!"

Hibbler shook his head again. "What a liar!"

They returned to the sheriff's office. Hibbler asked, "When is the trial, a few days?"

"Yes. We'll put you up at the hotel."

Hibbler looked satisfied. "I want to see him permanently behind bars."

"Or hung. With your testimony, the jury's got to find him guilty."

The trial itself took less than an hour. The jury went out and came in immediately with a guilty verdict.

But because Nate cooperated with the law, he was sentenced to twenty years in prison, instead of climbing to a hangman's platform.

Nate told them, "Reno's got piles of money stashed away at his mother's house in Lassiter."

"Money from robberies?"

"All of it. His mother's name is Haskins. Anybody in town can tell you where to find the house."

The sheriff sent two deputies to Lassiter with instructions to search the house till they found the cache.

Then Nate made a list of all the robberies he and Reno had been involved with over the years. And when that was finished, he was taken to prison.

It stormed again before Reno reached Lassiter, but the snow fell only in light flurries and the storm passed quickly, leaving behind frozen puddles and streams. There was no wind and he rode steadily, entering the little burg at night.

He put his horse in his mother's stable; she was astonished to see him. "Are you all right?"

"I'm fine. I just want to rest for a few days."

She did not inquire into his reasons. And when she went to the market for supplies, he unloaded the cement box and put the money in the stable. If the law showed up, he wanted to be ready to hightail it out.

But the law did not appear.

The money was in heavy rope-topped canvas sacks. He dug a deep hole in a corner of the stable, put the bags in a tin container in the hole, covered the container, and tamped the earth down carefully so it looked exactly the same as the rest of the stable floor. He carried the excess dirt out into the alley and scattered it thinly.

When he was finished, he stacked firewood over the spot, satisfied that no one would find it.

In mid-morning the next day, Reno had just poured out a cup of coffee when there was a rapping at the front door.

He jumped up, and his mother went to the door. Two deputies pushed their way in as she shouted at them, warning her son. Reno slid out the back, into the stable, and saddled his horse. When one of the deputies opened the back door, Reno fired twice at him, then galloped down the alley.

At the edge of town, he turned east into the hills, and it began to rain lightly.

The deputies were slow in following and lost him very quickly. Reno knew the hills and circled around to a spot where he could see the house. He stayed there the rest of the day. That night, when the deputies had gone, he went down to the house. The two men had searched every room, tearing into walls and wrecking furniture and cabinets. As Reno had expected, they had found the cement box—empty.

His mother had heard them talking. They had concluded that Reno had taken the money with him. They had returned to Calvin, with nothing.

Reno went back to Korning.

Chapter 18

Enoch Cobb was not entirely delighted to see Ki return to Korning—and his saloon. "If they find out I been boardin' you, they going to fix my wagon and plant me out in the goddamn sticks!"

"I don't want to put you at risk," Ki said. "I'll make my stay as short as I can. Is Reno Quant in town, do you know?"

"No, I don't know. But he hangs out at Heck Jennings's place. I can find out if he is."

"Thank you."

Enoch had newspapers, and Ki learned very quickly that Nate Tupper had been given a long prison sentence instead of hanging. Also, men discussed it in the bar. Most wondered why he'd been given a reduced sentence, and suspected he had told the law things it wanted to know.

A large amount of money had been taken with Nate, part of the reason he had been convicted. No dusty traveler or saddle tramp had thousands of dollars in his kick—that he could not explain.

Enoch knew all the merchants in town. Most of them

were not a part of the lawless element, but were forced to cater to it—shutting their eyes to the obvious fact that their money was tainted. A man did what he had to do. A few followed Enoch's example; he had the saloon up for sale, telling all who would listen that he wanted to retire to a porch in Nevers. And of course several prospective buyers came snooping through the rooms, and Ki had to vacate for the whiles . . .

Enoch quickly learned that Reno had just returned to Korning from a destination unknown, and was now in Heck Jennings's upstairs rooms. Gage Hindman was there as well. Would they recruit others to join the gang? A question no one could answer.

Of course not even Enoch dared ask too many questions, especially about Reno. A few did speculate, since winter was on the way out, what Reno had planned.

Ki waited and listened, but finally decided he had learned all he could. He thanked Enoch for his hospitality and left late at night for Levine.

Jessie was relieved to see him.

Heck Jennings supplied information when he could. He'd met a man recently come from Emitsville who had a plan to intercept the stage to Ebanville. He had discovered it carried gold and other treasure to merchants there.

Reno was interested. The man, Jeter Fisk, seemed to know what he was talking about. The treasure, when it was sent, was always secret, so no other guards were sent with it. It was in a strongbox, very like the Wells Fargo green boxes, and was picked up by the stage at the depot as ordinary baggage.

Reno asked him, "What you mean, 'when it's sent'?"

"Well, they don't send out treasure with ever' trip. You got to know which stage is carryin' it."

"And how you know that?"

Jeter grinned. "I been workin' at the stage line for goin' on eight months. B'now I know ever'thing that goes on. I know when they put the strongbox in the boot—they does it at night when nobody's around, so nobody sees it."

Heck said, "So Jeter will tell you which stage is carrying the box, and you do the rest. And you give him ten percent." He looked at Reno. "Is that agreed?"

Reno nodded. "How often they send this strongbox?"

"About once a week. They take the regular stage road like they been doin' for years."

Reno said, "What about you? You ain't on the job. They going to be suspicious and change ever'thing?"

Jeter shook his head. "They give me a week's leave to visit my folks in Nevers. My pa's sick."

Heck said, "Jeter's all right. He came to me with this opportunity. He's going back to Emitsville tonight."

They needed a signal, so Jeter suggested that he leave a broom in the window. "I sweep out the waiting room ever' morning. It's got one window. I'll leave a broom where you can see it by walkin' by. That means the strongbox is going out the next day on the noon stage. That all right?"

It was.

Jeter asked, "How I get my ten percent?"

"I'll send it to you," Heck promised.

The U.S. marshal's office was in Havelock. Jessie wrote a letter to the marshal, informing him that she had good information that Reno Quant was in Korning, suggesting that another raid might well bag him and Gage Hindman.

She received a reply from a chief clerk thanking her for the letter and explaining that the marshal's energies were taken up with cattle thefts. He was not available, but her letter would be read by him as soon as possible.

She sighed, saying to Ki, "We'll have to wait till Reno turns up again."

"He may decide to retire and walk the straight and narrow."

"How many crooks of Reno's caliber do that?"

Ki shrugged. "Maybe none. I have no idea. But if he does change his name and go off somewhere far away, we may never corral him. At the same time, I'd hate to hear that he's robbed and killed again . . ."

"We'd stop it if we could," Jessie said philosophically.

Reno and Gage rode to Emitsville, entering the town at night, an hour apart. They stayed at the same six-bit house, and Gage visited the stage-line waiting room daily, paying special attention to the window.

The second day after they arrived, the broom was there.

Gage hurried back to the hotel. "It'll be on the southbound stage tomorrow. We best hustle."

They saddled up and left town at once, taking the stage road south, looking for a good ambush spot. The land was fairly flat for a half dozen miles, and the road was straight as an arrow. Then it entered some low hills, turning and twisting to take the easiest course.

They found what they were looking for—a long climb up to a ridge. The road went straight up the hill, and over the ridge it drifted off to the south in a series of gentle curves.

"They'll go slow; the horses'll walk up the hill," Reno said. "We'll stop 'em near the top."

"Nothing to it." Gage grinned in anticipation.

"Don't shoot anybody 'less we have to," Reno warned. "They won't come after us hard then. Pull your wipe up over your face."

They made camp near the hill and sat on the slope in the thick brush next morning, waiting for the stage. It was on time, by Reno's watch. From the hill they could see for miles over the flats. The horses raised a dust cloud that followed the moving dots.

As they approached the hill, the horses slowed and began the long climb to the ridge. The stage was a Concord, painted blue and white, with six horses, a driver, and a shotgun messenger.

As the coach neared the top of the slope, Reno and Gage stepped out with rifles ready, one on either side of the road.

The driver hauled in on his lines, and the coach halted. He set the brake as Reno yelled, "Throw down that shotgun!"

The man looked at him, hesitated, then tossed it into the weeds.

The driver said, "We ain't got nothing but a few passengers."

Reno could see a few of them sticking their heads out, staring at him with round eyes. He said, "You got a strongbox. Let's have it."

The driver grunted. He tied the reins, climbed down, and unfastened the straps of the boot. Gage watched the passengers and the man on the seat. Reno looked into the boot; the box was there.

"Lift it out," he said, and the driver tugged and hauled it out and dropped it on the roadway. He looked at Reno.

Reno said, "All right. On your way." He motioned with the rifle.

The driver climbed to his seat again and took up the reins. He kicked off the brake and the coach moved. As Gage had said—nothing to it.

As the stage went down the opposite slope, Reno shot off the lock on the strongbox.

Inside there were packs of greenbacks in brown wrappers, and paper envelopes containing small pieces of jewelry. A sheaf of papers was tied together— lists of the items and the owners' names. Ignoring the papers, they quickly divided the money and envelopes, shoving them into saddlebags. They would count the money later.

Gage flung the strongbox into the brush, and they mounted and rode eastward. That was more like it.

The stagecoach was a day and a half on the road before it reached a way station with a telegraph. The news of the holdup went out, with descriptions of the bandits.

Jessie and Ki read the account posted on the bulletin board in the Emitsville telegraph office. It did not read like a Reno gang holdup.

"Nobody was shot," Ki said. "They didn't even rob the passengers."

"But from the descriptions, they could be Reno and Hindman. There were only two men."

"They knew about the strongbox. That sounds like Reno," Ki admitted. "But if it was Reno, how do you suppose he knew? We thought he was in Korning."

"He has informants," Jessie said. "Someone in Emitsville told him. How else?"

Ki nodded. "Let's talk to the stage-line manager. Maybe one of the clerks is taking money on the side."

The manager, Emory Beal, was a short, bespectacled man who had worked for the stage line most of his life. He did not want to believe one of his clerks or handlers was crooked.

"It's the most logical place for information about a secret parcel to originate," Jessie said. "I assume all your people here live in town . . ."

"Yes, of course. And none of them knows holdup men."

Ki asked, "Are all of them accounted for? All on the job?"

"Yes, certainly. You're barking up the wrong tree. Every one is—" He stopped suddenly and looked perplexed.

Jessie said, "What is it?"

135

"Everyone is accounted for, but one man is away at the moment, in Nevers. His father is sick."

"When will he be back?"

"He's due in tomorrow."

"What's his name?"

"Jeter Fisk. He's a handyman."

"Is he married?"

"No."

Jessie said, "We'll be here in the morning to talk to him. Please say nothing to him about us."

"Very well . . ."

Jeter Fisk was a skinny, shifty-eyed young man who was almost surly when they confronted him in the stage-line barn the next day. No, he knew nothing about the holdup—how could he?

Ki said, "You knew when the money shipment went out."

"I wasn't the only one!"

"You told Mr. Beal you went to Nevers to see your father?"

"Yes. He's in bed, sick."

"And you did nothing else? You went there and came directly back here?"

Jeter stiffened. "What am I, a child? You got no right to question me like this."

"Answer the question," Ki said evenly.

"What question?"

Jessie smiled. "You went to Nevers, you said. Where else did you go?"

"No place else! I went there and come back here."

She insisted. "You're sure you went nowhere else?"

"No! I come right back here."

Ki said, "And you told no one about the shipment?"

"That's right. Nobody."

They left Jeter to do his chores in the barn. As they walked to the street, Jessie said, "Did you believe him?"

"I'm afraid not. But we'll have to go to Nevers to prove it, one way or the other."

"I think so, too. Let's go."

★

Chapter 19

The weather stayed good, warming a little more each day. The road had just been log-scraped; there was considerable traffic between the two towns. They were able to take the stage and arrive in Nevers about dusk of the second day.

Ki questioned a number of people, and they easily found the Fisk home. Jessie rapped on the door, and it was opened by an elderly man who was obviously surprised to see her.

She asked, "Are you Mr. Fisk?"

"Yes, I am . . ."

"Are you Jeter's father, sir?"

"Yes." A puzzled look.

She smiled. "You don't look sick to me."

"Sick? I'm not sick. What's this about Jeter? Has something happened to him?"

"No. He's fine. But he told us you were sick in bed. Have you seen him lately?"

"No. We ain't seen him for a year." The older man frowned. "He told you I was sick?" He stared from her to Ki by the hitchrack in front of the house. "Who are you all anyways?"

Jessie smiled sweetly. "The stage line sent us. Jeter works for the line, and he took a few days off that he wasn't supposed to, that's all."

"And he said he come here?"

"Yes."

Fisk sighed deeply. "That kid—he allus was easy with the truth. Is he in trouble?"

"That's up to the manager. Thank you for your time, sir." She went back to the horse.

As they rode away, she told Ki what had been said. "Jeter didn't come here. He went somewhere else. Do you suppose he met Reno?"

"I'd guess he met Reno—or some other holdup man. I can't see Jeter holding up a stage, can you?"

"Of course there were two of them . . ."

"But Jeter doesn't come anywhere near to fitting the description of either."

"That's right."

The money added up to slightly more than three thousand dollars. They counted it at sundown in a copse of trees, and Reno put aside three hundred for Heck. "He can give Jeter what he wants . . ."

It was a bit more than Reno had expected. There were also some legal papers, which Gage used to make a fire. They looked at the jewelry, brooches, earrings, pendants, and rings. Neither of them had the slightest idea of values. The stones might be expensive and they might be glass. The settings were probably gold . . . In the end, they divided them and put them into saddlebags. Some hooker would probably be glad to get them.

Then they rode back to Korning.

When they paid Heck back what they had borrowed,

the take was whittled down. They needed another plan. But Heck had nothing for them; no one had come to him with a proposition. He could only suggest they ride around and look at banks.

Reno sat in his room with a cigar and stared out the grimy window. Robbing banks could be a dangerous business—depending on the bank. Some had much better security than others. He recalled going into one or two banks in the past, after looking them over well, he thought, and being surprised by hidden guns. A man could get dead that way.

What he wanted was another Army payroll. That had been fast and easy, with very little danger attached. A good ambush was always to be desired.

He grunted and dumped ashes on the floor. That kind of job did not come along every day.

The sudden deaths of Sonny and Vince, and Nate being in prison, made him feel edgy also. He had always known it could happen anytime, but it had been quick for both. Only a short time ago there had been five of them. Now they were down to two. Gage felt much the same way, he knew. Who would be next?

Reno puffed the cigar. Stop thinking that way. It was nothing more than luck—their luck had run out. He could still hear the sickening thump as Sonny's body hit the floor of the merchantile building. It had been dumb luck that Sonny had gone down the rope first. Reno had had it in mind to lead the way—and he could not say why he had let Sonny go first. Just luck.

But stop thinking about that.

What to do now? The good weather would not last forever.

Confronted with the fact that he had not gone to Nevers at all, with Emory Beal glaring at him, Jeter confessed that he had traveled to Korning and met Reno Quant. He needed money, Jeter said, as if it were an excuse.

Reno had done the holdup, promising him ten percent—which he had not received. He did not know where Reno had gone after the holdup. Probably back to Korning.

He was put into the local hoosegow to await the circuit judge.

It did not help them much, as Ki said. They were no closer to Reno.

Korning was full of hardcases, and Heck Jennings put out the word that he was interested in opportunities. Miles Oliver heard it and came round to the saloon to see him.

"Cows," Miles said. He was a rangy, weathered man in checked shirt and jeans who, he said, had been in the cattle business most of his life, one way or another. Ranchers to the south brought herds to Denning on the railroad. They came twice a year, spring and fall.

"Cows?" Heck said in surprise. "What're you talking about?"

They sat in a corner of the saloon in mid-morning while several men were sweeping out and cleaning up after the night's imbibing. Miles leaned over the table. "They brings the cows to Denning to sell 'em. Buyers come there with money. Cash on the barrelhead."

"Ahhhh, I see," Heck said.

"I need two men t'throw in with me. We ought to git us twenty, thirty thousand easy."

"Two men? Reno and Hindman are looking for something like that."

"Reno?" Miles grunted. "He's too damn quick to shoot. I dunno about Reno."

"What's worrying you?"

Miles made a face. "You shoot people, the law comes after you harder. The Pinkertons is thicker'n horseflies out

141

there now. I don't think I want Reno."

"He's not stupid. Talk to him."

Miles shook his shaggy head. "I hear he's a mite short-tempered, too. You talk to him and tell me. All right?"

Heck shrugged. "All right."

"But let's do 'er soon. Them cows will be sold and the buyers gone if we diddle daddle."

"I understand."

Heck took Reno aside, telling him what Miles had said. "It sounds like a high-paying proposition. Cattle are selling for twenty dollars according to the papers."

Reno was interested. "Bring him up to the room."

Heck hesitated. "I've been thinking about it. Do you need him, you and Gage? You can find out where the buyers hang out and go to them when they're looking the other way."

Reno nodded. "I been there. Denning's a small burg. It ought to be easy."

"All right. I'll stall Miles a few days." Heck rolled a cigar in his fingers. "What you say?"

"Sounds likely. We'll leave in the morning."

They left before sunup and rode south and east. They reached Osage Creek in late afternoon of the second day and followed it a long trip into Denning.

It was a small, teeming town, busy with cattlemen and cowhands, a few townspeople and merchants, girls in second-floor windows, yelling down to those in the street, and cattle in pens, bawling. Reno and Gage went boldly into town, and no one paid them any attention.

Cattle buyers were easy to find; they had newly painted signs tacked to the fronts of buildings. A few were in hastily erected tents; some alongside tents where newly arrived girls worked at their trade.

Reno visited several saloons, listening to the gossip. Only two herds had arrived so far, he heard. They had quickly been sold and the hands paid off. Some had gone home; some were still celebrating the end of trail. But another herd was on the horizon and would be in the pens in another day. Some of the buyers had ridden out to deal with the trail boss . . . Business was booming.

The town buildings were old and shacky, and Reno saw no safes in any of the offices. Cattle buying was not a lingering kind of business. A herd appeared, was counted and sold and shipped out on waiting cars immediately, to make way for other herds. When the herds were gone, the buyers would disappear, too.

He saw five different cattle buyers, according to the signs. All men of experience. He watched them at the cattle pens with the trail bosses. They talked and prodded, then walked down the street to the office to sign papers, and went from there to the bank. The money was paid over to the cattleman, and he and his hands went off to their camp on the prairie.

The buyer had no money in his office. It was all paid over at the bank. The bank had two shotgun guards in plain sight.

Gage wanted to figure a way to get into the bank, but Reno thought that was foolishness. "This goddamn town is full of cowhands. Ever' one of them trigger-itchy."

"Then what the hell can we do?"

"This here was a piss-poor idea. That drifter didn't know what the hell he was talking about. And if we rob the trail boss, we got us the same problem, wild-shootin' cowhands on our tails. They prob'ly worse than a posse." Reno was disgusted.

Gage said, "You wanna give it all up?"

Reno nodded. "The odds is terrible. Let's git the hell out'n here."

• • •

When they started back, it began to rain. Reno cursed the weather and swore the entire time that everything had gone wrong from the beginning. It was a stupid idea, trying to rob cattle buyers—it couldn't be done. They had figured out foolproof ways to protect themselves long ago. Miles Oliver was an idiot, and they never should have listened to him.

The rain continued, never letting up, even at night, and it grew colder. By the time they reached Korning, they were both sodden, half-frozen and miserable, tired to death of the long ride that had gained them nothing . . . Nothing would please them.

Reno huddled before a blazing fire with a bottle, then piled into bed and refused to talk to anyone.

Heck Jennings learned from Gage what a disaster the trip had been. Everything had gone wrong; the buyers were impossible to hold up. Gage advised Heck to keep Miles Oliver out of Reno's way.

"He left town," Heck said.

"Lucky for him."

Reno had the girl Vivi sent up to his room and spent half the next day with her, and in her, and it softened his disposition a bit, and that evening Heck went to his room.

"You in a mood to talk?"

"Talk about what?"

"About a business in Dakins. You been in that town?"

"Yes . . ."

"Did you notice the brickyard? It's a big place out on the south end of town."

"Naw." Reno shook his head.

"Well, they say it's the biggest in the territory, maybe this half of the country. It got a big payroll."

"Ahhhh," Reno said. "Payroll is a nice-soundin' word."

He poured out a large dollop of brandy. "How d'you know about this place?"

"A drifter told me while you was gone. Said he worked there a month or so, drivin' a wagon. They bring the cash payroll from the bank in town to the brickyard ever' Friday."

"Lemme talk to this drifter."

Heck shook his head. "He went on east a couple days ago. But I got a plan of the brickyard from him." Heck unfolded a paper. He pointed with his finger. "These here are the offices. This is a kiln—"

"What's that?"

"An oven. They bake the bricks in it. It's got a big chimney. Over here is the drying yards—but all you got to know is the office. That's where they deliver the money. They pay off in cash every Friday."

"They's two buildings there. Which one is the office?"

"The one with the sign out front: Dakin Brickyard. The cashier's office is just inside to the left. It got a sign on it, too."

"The money that comes from the bank. Does it come the same time every Friday?"

Heck made a face. "I forgot to ask that."

Reno grunted. "The longer we sit in that damn cashier's office, the bigger the chances. Who brings the money?"

"A bank clerk and a deputy. The money's in a carpetbag or a leather satchel."

"How much money?"

"Maybe a thousand dollars or more, depending."

"Depending on what?"

"Sometimes they got to buy new machinery or get something repaired, or pay for supplies . . . Lots of things make a difference."

Reno took the plan to his room and frowned over it. There were a few unknowns, but in general it looked easy.

Of course the take wasn't much, nothing like the Army payroll had been, but a thousand dollars was a thousand dollars.

Studying the crude map, he wondered if he might do the job alone, without Gage. If so, he wouldn't have to split. But if the drifter who had made the map was wrong, and if there were five men delivering the money instead of two—well, he'd let them deliver it.

Too, there could be other important details lacking. No, he might need Gage's gun.

★

Chapter 20

Enoch Cobb finally sold his saloon in Korning and came to Levine with a wagon bearing all his worldly goods. Jessie and Ki met him in the hotel. He looked much better, more at ease. The life in Korning, an outlaw town, had been a strain. He was happy to be shut of it at last.

However, he had news of Reno. A drifter in the saloon had told him he'd sold Heck Jennings a plan, and Jennings had mentioned he'd give it to Reno.

"A plan of what?" Jessie asked.

"A brickyard."

She smiled. "Why would Reno want a plan of a brickyard?"

Enoch grinned. "It's a big place with a big payroll."

"Of course," Ki said. "Where is this brickyard?"

"Jesus," Enoch said, "I forgot to ask him."

"Well, how many brickyards are there in the territory anyway? We ought to be able to find it."

Ki said, "I don't remember ever seeing a brickyard this side of Kansas City."

"The local paper might know," Jessie said.

"I'll go and ask," Ki agreed.

He talked to a man in a green eyeshade in the newspaper office.

"A brickyard?" the editor said. "Certainly. There's one at Dakins. I believe it's the only one west of the Missouri."

"Thank you . . ."

They left for the town immediately. Enoch could not say how fresh his news was. The robbery might already have taken place.

Dakins was a settled town of more than four thousand souls. It had started as an Army fort; the town grew up around the fort, which had been abandoned by the Army some twenty years before.

It consisted of a central town and a wide scattering of houses and shacks on poorly defined streets without names. It was in a pleasant valley, on a stage line, and had recently been the county seat.

On arriving, Jessie and Ki went at once to view the brickyard, a cluster of once-painted buildings behind a wire fence just outside the town. Smoke came from three tall chimneys, and the place looked perfectly peaceful and busy. As they watched, a loaded wagon came from the yard and turned south on the road out of town.

Ki said, "We'd best talk to the sheriff . . ."

The sheriff was a man named Ty Uber who had very recently defeated Tom Landon in the election. He looked like a town alderman, pudgy and middle-aged, pale as an egg. What had he promised in order to win?

He listened to them and squirmed in his chair when he heard Reno's name.

"You say you think Reno's gang is coming here?"

Jessie nodded. "Yes. We do."

"But you don't know when?"

Ki said, "There's no way we could know exactly. We assume it will be soon."

Uber frowned. "That's not much to go on, is it? And this office has other problems . . ."

Jessie asked, "Will you warn the people at the brickyard?"

"The yard is owned by Isaiah Larch, one of the hardest heads this side of Cleveland. He was for Tom Landon in the election. He isn't going to listen to me. You want to talk to him, go ahead—with my blessing." He shook his head. "But you're wasting your time."

"Thanks, Sheriff . . ."

They went along the boardwalk, and Ki said, "We can't count on him. If the brickyard is robbed, he'd probably laugh."

"Yes, he might. So—we do it alone. How do you suppose Reno will do the robbery?"

"Interesting question. He may wait in the brickyard office for the money to come to him, or he may intercept the messengers."

Jessie said, "I think he'll intercept."

"Why?"

"Because he doesn't know when the money will arrive, and he won't want to wait—it might come with a posse."

Ki nodded. "I think so, too. Let's look at the route. The money will start from the bank."

The Dakins Union Bank was in the center of town, a red-brick two-story building with a black iron awning over the walk in front of it.

Ki said, "If I were delivering the money, I'd go along the main street as far as I could . . . with people all around."

They walked from the bank to where they could see the brickyard chimneys. The yard was off the road nearly a half mile. Several streets led toward it, with buildings, homes, corrals, and shacks along the way, and wide, weedy fields between the buildings.

Jessie said, "If we're right, they'll go down one of these streets to the yard."

"Yes." Ki gazed down the road that led out of town. "And if they do the holdup here, they'll have a big jump on a posse."

"You know—they've been sending the payroll to the yard on Fridays. Why don't we suggest they vary the day?"

"Good idea! Why don't we see if we can talk to Mr. Larch today? We won't tell him we've talked to the sheriff."

The brickyard was surrounded by a dusty wire fence. The gate was sturdy, wire and iron, standing open for the wagons. No one stopped them as they went in and up the steps to the office building. A stout woman clerk asked them their business and led them to a door marked, "Isaiah Larch, Pres."

She rapped, opened the door an inch or two, and said, "Visitors, Mr. Larch."

"Bring 'em in."

Larch was a big man. He got up from behind an untidy desk and stretched. He was in shirtsleeves and suspenders. He took off his specs and dropped them on the desk papers, gazing with interest at Jessie.

"Sit down, folks. What can I do f'you?"

Ki said, "We've come with a warning, sir."

"A warning? What you mean?"

Jessie added, "We think you're in danger of being robbed, Mr. Larch."

The big man stared at them. "Izzat so?" He did not look alarmed. "Robbed of what?"

"Your payroll."

"Ahh." Larch nodded, eyes squinting at them. "Why d'you think so?"

Jessie asked, "Do you know who Reno Quant is?"

"I've heard the name. He's a bandit?"

"We think he's coming here to rob you. Your payroll

comes from the bank every Friday . . ."

Larch nodded. "Ever' Friday morning. Guarded by a deputy. Costs me a dollar f'him. We never had any trouble—"

Jessie said, "You're likely to have trouble soon. We suggest you change the day to Thursday."

The big man frowned. "I ain't got a safe to put the money in."

Ki said, "Maybe you could conceal it overnight."

Larch squinted at him, saying nothing. Finally he nodded and got to his feet. "Good of you all to come and see me . . ."

Jessie gave him her best smile and went to the door. Larch hurried to open it for her and ushered them out.

As they went down the steps, Ki said, "I feel as if I've just been patted on the head and told to be a good boy."

She laughed. "You think he didn't believe us?"

"I think he's a man who will do things his way, no matter what. The sheriff is right. He's a hardhead."

"Well, after all, it must be a shocker to be told you're about to be robbed. I suppose we'll have to see what he does. There's no way he can be forced to be sensible."

In Dakins, Reno studied the brickyard and decided to stick to his original plan. There was no way he could tell how many people were employed at the yard; since the drifter had disappeared, there was no one to ask. But it might be easy to get bottled up in the office if he waited there. It would be better to bushwhack the messengers somewhere in the town, where there were plenty of escape routes handy.

He and Gage had arrived in Dakins on a Wednesday and taken rooms in a boardinghouse well off the main drag, telling the owner they were just passing through on their way north. They would rest up a few days, then go on.

On Friday morning they were both sitting on benches along the main street near the bank, with half a dozen others, mostly old-timers who were enjoying the sun. They watched a mounted deputy arrive, go into the bank, and come out minutes later with a portly man who looked like a clerk.

The stout man carried a satchel and had to struggle to mount a skittish bay horse. He finally got seated, and the two walked the horses along the busy street, the deputy with a Winchester across his thighs.

Reno and Gage got up casually and followed on foot. Gage crossed the street to be sure no one noticed them together. They had no trouble keeping the two riders in view. Reno paused, watching the two turn down a side street, no more than a weed-edged lane, that led to the brickyard.

He lit a cigar and waited, leaning against a shack as if he belonged there. In about ten minutes, the two men came from the brickyard office, got on their horses, and rode back into town. The place to ambush them was at the turning, by the old shack.

When he and Gage met up again, Reno said, "We'll hit 'em when they turn off the main street. We grab the satchel and hightail it down the road south. We ought to have a half hour's start at the least. Maybe more, if they mill around some."

"Where d'you figger we ought to go?"

"I think we ought to split up quick, soon's we get out of sight. We can meet in Marshfield. All right?"

Gage nodded.

Jessie and Ki talked to the young deputy assigned to guard the brickyard payroll, telling him their fears, that Reno Quant might be in town.

Ki asked him, "What about more deputies?"

"We ain't got 'em."

The deputy was a skinny man of some twenty years; he was obviously startled to hear about Reno, but bound to do his duty. He refused to allow Jessie and Ki to accompany him, saying it was not a fit job for a woman. Jessie had heard this many times, but did not argue.

Ki asked the young man to vary the route, if nothing else, and the deputy agreed. So that on the following Friday morning, the deputy and the bank clerk turned down another side street, one before the lane they'd taken the previous week.

Reno and Gage were waiting at the wrong corner, concealed in the shack. When they realized what was happening, they piled on their horses and galloped after the messengers in a fury.

Hearing the hoofbeats, the deputy slammed shots at them with his rifle. Jessie and Ki joined the fracas, also firing at the would-be bandits, who suddenly broke away and galloped all out, across a weedy field to the south road.

Jessie and Ki were perhaps a half mile behind when Reno and Gage reached the road.

Reno swore when he realized the messengers had taken another route. And when he and Gage rushed after, and the deputy opened fire at them, he knew the game was up. It was a botched job—now the only thing to do was get out fast! They galloped across the field, gained the road, and sped down it with bullets flying past.

What had happened? Was it luck—or had the local sheriff learned they were going to grab the payroll? It was probably luck, Reno thought. Else there would have been more deputies.

Two others had fired at them also, but too far back for him and Gage to see in their hurry.

In a dozen minutes, they entered a wooden area, and out

of sight of the pursuers, Reno yelled to Gage to go left. He would go right, and they'd meet later.

Gage waved and turned away at once.

They lost sight of the two in the trees, and Jessie and Ki slowed, approaching the wood, fearing an ambush. But there was none. Ki took the lead with Jessie following in single file, both walking their horses.

Ki leaned down, looking for tracks on the hard ground. They went several miles before he suddenly halted and slid to the ground and knelt, brushing away leaves. He looked very annoyed.

"They've split up!"

Jessie looked back. "How long ago?"

"I can't tell. I'm not that good a tracker. But we're following one man, no telling which one."

"Damn," Jessie said.

Ki leaned on his horse. "We've got no choice, have we? We'll have to keep on after this one."

"Well, they'll probably meet somewhere—previously agreed to, don't you think?"

"I'm sure of it." Ki nodded. He mounted and turned the horse's head. "We'll keep after this one then."

"I hope it's Reno," Jessie said.

★

Chapter 21

Gage knew he was being followed, and he did his best to throw off his pursuers without losing his lead, but the ground, though hard in places, was generally soft from the recent rains. His best bet was to keep ahead of them.

He had no binoculars, so it was impossible to tell who they were. He had to assume they were lawmen. Possibly a couple of young hell-for-leather deputies, wanting to make names for themselves, had seen what happened at the old shack and come after him and Reno. And by dumb luck they happened to follow him, with Reno off the hook.

He halted just before dusk, over the summit of a low ridge, and crawled back to scan his backtrail. Were there two riders back there—or not? The light was going fast, and he could not be sure. He had better not stop for the night.

There was no moon and it was dark. When he came to a rippling stream, he halted to fill his canteen and let the roan horse drink. Then he crossed and walked the animal a mile or more before mounting again. He made poor time at night, in unfamiliar country, and when dawn came again, he was weary and red-eyed.

He looked at the sky, not at all sure where he was. Marshfield was certainly somewhere off to his right and south, but pinpointing it was impossible; he would have to guess. Maybe when he got closer, he'd run onto a road. He kept bending toward the right, then worried that he'd turned too far.

But he had another worry—food. He'd come without anything at all, and now he was ravenous. He unbitted his horse and let the animal graze for a while, then went on. Maybe his pursuers were in the same boat. He sincerely hoped so.

Then, in the middle of the day, as he crossed a small, rounded hill, a shot came sizzling out of the prairie behind him. It was followed by two more before he could spur the roan. The shots came from a long way off but were uncomfortably close. He was still being followed.

Were they letting him know it?

Ki was very confident. "He's leaving an easy trail to follow, not trying to hide a thing—not taking any time to try."

"He's not moving in a straight line either," Jessie said. She glanced at the sun. "He's much farther west than he was. Is that deliberate?"

"Probably. If he's going to meet the other one. What's south of here?"

"Marshfield, for one."

"Marshfield . . . that's a big place. We'd be better off to stop him before he gets there—if we can."

Jessie shaded her eyes. Nothing moved in front of them.

Ki said, "Maybe we can put him afoot . . . A lucky shot . . ."

They got a chance to do that the next day as their quarry crossed a low hill. Ki fired three shots at the distant horse— but missed.

156

Jessie said cheerfully, "Well, now he knows for sure we're here."

"He knew already. If we can keep him moving, give him no chance to rest, we might get close enough."

"It'll give *us* no chance to rest either."

Ki smiled. "I'm counting on the hope that we have more stamina."

"Let's do it then."

Ki got in another shot toward late afternoon. The fleeing man was halted, and the bullet spanged off a rock beside him—and he suddenly disappeared. When they arrived at the spot, they saw he had ducked into an arroyo. His tracks in the damp sand led south.

They were definitely closer to him. Maybe his horse was tiring. But the closer they came, as Ki mentioned several times, the more danger there was that he would turn and lay in wait for them. And that fact slowed them.

Gage thought of it often—ambushing the two pursuers. But he hated to let them get that close. Two riflemen were dangerous—even if he surprised them. He might get one of them, but the other might get *him* at the same time. He had heard talk about smokeless powder—what a help that would be! But there was no such thing, and maybe never would be.

He loped the roan horse along the arroyo for more than a mile, then found an easy path up out of it as the arroyo swung off to the east. The land began to turn hilly and more ragged, which he welcomed; it would make his pursuers more cautious.

The weather had been pleasant, but now it, too, began to change. Low clouds came scudding out of the west, thin, filmy stuff at first, but leading more sturdy, roiling, and darker clouds. And it got colder.

By nightfall the thick clouds were overhead, seeming

157

to press down, and a clammy fog accompanied them, at treetop level, sending writhing tendons everywhere.

Gage continued, walking the horse, expecting rain any moment. A chilly mist settled around him, and then the rain came at last, pattering down in huge drops, and he stopped in a thick grove, huddling in the saddle, feeling his stomach churning. God, he was hungry!

Thunder rumbled in the distance, and he could see darts of lightning; the thunder gradually came nearer. It was probably one of the last storms of the season, and just in time to help him. He ought to be able to evade them now. The rain would cover his tracks.

He wanted to go on—the sooner he reached some kind of civilization, the sooner he'd find food. But the rain came down very hard, and he stayed where he was, comforted by the fact that his pursuers would be holed up, too.

The thick branches of the trees were some shelter, turning much of the storm. He was cold and miserable, on top of being famished. He thought about starting a fire but gave up the idea. It would probably be impossible. He suffered the rain and cold for hours, trying not to think about sitting down in a restaurant . . . Had he ever been so hungry?

When the rain let up toward morning, he left the trees and went south in a drizzle, shaking uncontrollably. He came to a swollen stream that had overflowed its banks and was carrying brush and weeds, swirling brown water that looked deep. It was too wide and swift to cross, so he went along beside it for miles, till it swung eastward into sodden lowlands.

That afternoon, on high ground, he examined his backtrail carefully and could see no one following. He waited a half hour, but no rider appeared in the distance. Had he lost them? Maybe they had gotten tired of it, the weather and all, and gone back. He hoped so.

How far was Marshfield? He had no idea. He was in

a desolate part of the land; maybe no one had trod this ground ever before.

And then toward evening he came on a fieldstone house— or part of one. Three walls were standing and a tiny part of a roof. It was a one-room affair that looked as if it had been slowly decaying for years. Gage cleared away some of the debris—there was plenty of firewood—and made a fire in the fireplace; it was intact except for a chimney. The fire warmed him, but did nothing for his hunger.

He was beginning to feel light-headed. His hands shook, and he was definitely weaker. In the morning, it was worse. He managed to climb on the roan horse and head south, chewing a bit of leather.

And he began to feel that he didn't care about the pursuers—let them come. Maybe they would give him food.

Ki lost the tracks near the ruin of the stone house. The ground was very hard, and even though he got down on his hands and knees, he could find no sign.

He said to Jessie, "He may have gone on south, or— if he noticed the ground—he might have turned abruptly east or west. If we continue south, we may lose him for good."

"What's your best guess?"

"I think we should go on a mile or two and see if we cut sign. If not, we can always return here and maybe get lucky."

"Yes. Let's do it."

Two or three miles farther on, the ground changed and the tracks were plain. Ki breathed a sigh of relief. As he had confessed to Jessie, he was not the best tracker, and he had feared that the pursued had given them the slip.

But they had lost hours of time.

Much later in the day, Jessie noticed smoke on the horizon. "Is it a prairie fire?"

But as they came closer, it was obvious the smoke came from a chimney. And the tracks led straight to it. As they came to a ridge, they saw it was a stone house with a corral, close by a stream.

A hand-painted sign on the door said, "Trading Post, P. Sayre, Prop."

Ki slid off the horse. "Let me go close. If it's Reno inside, he'll shoot on sight." He made a wide circle approaching the house from the side, where there was only one small window, high up.

Then, *shuriken* in hand, he slid through the door—but came out a moment later to motion Jessie to come. The man they pursued was not here.

"They was a feller here," the proprietor, Sayre, said. "Bought him some vittles and a bottle of brandy and took off fast. Said he was hungry as a wolf."

Ki asked, "What did he look like?"

Sayre described Gage Hindman as Jessie and Ki looked at each other.

The trading-post owner was a middle-aged man, stooped with arthritis, but strong and clear-eyed. He'd lived alone since his wife died two years past, he told them.

"I'm thinkin' of pullin' up stakes and goin' back to Marshfield."

"How far is Marshfield?"

"Damn near a day's ride, straight south. Big town. That fella you want is headin' for it, sure."

"Yes. We think so, too."

They bought food from him and went on within the hour.

The trading post had saved his life, Gage thought. When he'd reached it, he wanted to slide down and collapse and not move for a week. But he forced himself to buy a sackful of food—more than he'd need for one day's ride—then climb back on the roan horse and leave.

He didn't mention the pursuers to the owner, Sayre, who wanted him to stay overnight. Sayre didn't get that many visitors. But Gage made an excuse and went on.

Marshfield was so close now . . .

Reno Quant went the opposite way when he and Gage split up, and he quickly realized he was not followed. The deputies, or whoever they were, had gone after Gage, which made him chuckle.

He rode across the open prairie and made excellent time, but he had no food either, and he was desperately hungry after the second day. There was a small town in his direction, he knew, and he began looking for it.

He saw smoke finally as he stood on a hillock, and headed for it. It was a tiny crossroads burg containing possibly fifty people all told, he thought. Half of them hardcases. He counted five shacky buildings, the largest of which was a saloon-mercantile store all in one.

He got down in front of it and walked in. There were six men in the large room, counting the owner, who wore an apron. They sat around tables and were gabbing till they heard Reno. They stopped talking and craned their necks to look.

The man in the long apron said, "Howdy."

Reno nodded. The men at the tables looked like hardcases all right. He said, "I'm on my way to Marshfield. I figger I go straight south. That right?"

"Yep. Pretty much. They's no road, though."

Reno looked at the shelves. "I need some vittles . . ." He pretended to pay no attention to the man who got up and went out quickly.

He asked, "What's the name of this place?"

"Odell." The owner fished under the counter and found a gunnysack. "What you want?"

Reno pointed to the shelf. "I'll take some of them peaches and a box of crackers—you got any cheese?"

The clerk uncovered a thick slab and picked up a knife. He placed it on the cheese. "This much?"

"A little more . . . yeah." He also bought a flat bottle of whiskey and put all the purchases in the gunnysack. He paid the bill, nodded to those around the tables, and went out to the horse. He tied the sack on, looking around casually, and mounted. The man who had gone out had been a tall, hawk-nosed citizen in a dark red shirt under a brown coat. He was nowhere in sight.

Riding past the buildings, he pointed south at a walk. When he was well past, he pulled each revolver in turn, opened the loading gate, and rolled the cylinder down his arm, looking at the brass. Loaded. He made sure the Winchester was loaded as well. Had Hawk-nose decided to ambush him?

The prairie was reasonably flat and the sky clear; he could see for miles in all directions. He did not move in a straight line and kept a close watch, even behind him. He laid the rifle across his thighs. There was little doubt in his mind that Hawk-nose might try to gun him down for the horse and saddle and what he had on him. He was better dressed than the average drifter, and someone in a little two-bit burg like Odell might figure he was in tall cotton.

But as far as he could see, nothing moved on the ground. Far off, a couple of hawks circled and swooped, busy making a living. He wondered all at once what had become of Gage. If the deputies had chased him, had they caught him? And if they had, would they be able to squeeze information out of him? Maybe something to the effect that he, Reno, was heading for Marshfield? He knew the police used rubber hoses now and again . . .

So it was possible.

But then, of course, Gage would not be taken easily, and he was not helpless.

He told himself, Forget Gage. Think about your own predicament. Hawk-nose hadn't had time to go very far from the little town—so he must be close by. And maybe with one or two others . . .

His head was turned when the first shot came from his right—then three more very fast. He glimpsed the smoke drifting and felt several of the shots hit the horse. The animal grunted and went down heavily, kicking as another shot hit.

Reno rolled free and scuttled behind the mound of the horse with the Winchester, swearing a blue streak. The ambusher had put him afoot! Hawk-nose must be in an arroyo that he hadn't noticed. It was a good sixty yards distant. He pulled his hat off and peered at the area he thought the shots had come from. A bunch of taller weeds marked the spot.

Sliding the rifle out, he aimed carefully and put a bullet into the middle of the weeds, ducking back instantly. He stared at the sky. How long till dark? Probably three or four hours. And he was pinned down. There was little possibility that he could jump up and run anywhere without getting hit. He sighed deeply. The best place for him was here, using the dead horse for a fort. Damnation!

No more shots came, seeking him. No rifle bullet would go through a horse. Probably Hawk-nose was waiting patiently for a good shot, knowing he couldn't stay behind the horse forever. Sooner or later . . .

It began to get dark, and Reno laid both revolvers in front of him—in case Hawk-nose charged. Maybe there were two of them, and they were even now creeping up on either side . . . But he couldn't see or hear anything.

163

The ground was flat; he'd see them if they tried it—while it was still light.

When it got dark, he moved. He slipped away, back, from the horse and circled around to the arroyo a hundred yards or more from where the other had fired on him.

He moved down the arroyo as silently as possible, a revolver in each hand—and came on the body. Hawk-nose was sprawled in the dirt with a red hole in his forehead!

Reno grunted in surprise. He had hit the other with his first shot! "You poor son of a bitch," he said.

Chapter 22

Jessie and Ki entered Marshfield without ever catching sight of Gage. Instead of a hotel, they chose a boardinghouse in the center of the city. Where had Gage gone? Probably to a prearranged meeting place—if he were meeting Reno.

The main drag was perhaps a half mile long, with stores, saloons and hurdy-gurdy houses, a few vacant lots, liveries, and banks along both sides of the wide street. They arrived on a Friday, and the town was busy. They stopped at the office of the marshal, Karl Hopkins, who looked his surprise at seeing them.

"You two still hunting Reno Quant?"

"Yes, we are," Jessie said. "We think he may come here—or already be here."

"That so . . ." Hopkins frowned. "I heard Nate Tupper got a long jail sentence."

"He did," Ki replied. "He'll be an old man when he gets out. Cross him off."

Hopkins said, "What're you two doing here in town? You got wind of something?"

"We're chasing Gage Hindman," Jessie said. "We think

he came here, unless he fooled us completely. He could have gone around the town."

Ki said, "We think he's meeting Reno. That's a guess, of course."

The marshal nodded. "When you deal with outlaws, much of it is a guess." He leaned back in his office chair. "If you do get word of Reno, let me know. I want him as bad as you do."

Jessie doubted that statement but did not argue.

The marshal's office was large, on one side of a hall that led to the jail in the rear of the building. Jessie was astonished when Scott Pelter came through the door. He was about to speak to Hopkins when he realized there were others in the room. He turned and faced Jessie, and his jaw dropped. "Jessie! Where did you come from! And Ki!" He shook hands with them. "God! It's good to see you both!"

"We're still chasing Reno," Jessie said, delighted to see him.

"Reno! I'd forgotten all about him."

"We think he may be here in town." Jessie wanted to throw her arms about him, but of course . . .

Scott glanced at Hopkins. "Reno here? Is that possible?"

"If Miss Starbuck says it is, then it is," he said gallantly.

She explained quickly about the aborted brickyard payroll attempt and how they had followed Gage Hindman, who was apparently making for Marshfield.

Scott said, "But you don't *know* that Reno was coming here . . ."

"That's true." Jessie smiled. "But he has to be somewhere."

Scott laughed and looked at his watch. "Come along, you two. Let's have lunch. We've a lot to catch up on."

Reno found the dead man's horse fifty yards farther on, tied to a bush in the arroyo. He pulled off the saddle and went back for his own. In half an hour he was on his way again. The horse was a bay and wanted to run. They climbed out of the arroyo, and Reno gave the animal its head.

In two days he came to Red Willow River and followed it into Marshfield, making sure he arrived late at night. He and Gage had agreed to meet at the Osage Saloon, which was run by an old friend, Grady Harris, who had not always been settled and honest.

Grady had bought the saloon several years back with money he'd stashed away before he went to jail. Now he was going reasonably straight. He knew that Karl Hopkins had kept an eye on him for a year or so, but had never nosed out anything illegal and now paid him no further attention.

Reno tied the bay in the back alley by the privies and went inside to Grady's office across from the storeroom.

Grady was astonished to see him. "Reno! By all that's holy! I thought you was dead."

"Why would you think that?" Reno locked the door behind him.

"Because you allus owlhootin' around, shootin' people." Grady found a bottle and two glasses. "Damn! It's a sight f'sore eyes, seein' you!" He poured into the glasses and gave Reno one. "Here's to old times."

They touched glasses and drank. Reno sat down and fished for his last cigar. "You got a place for me to hole up for a spell?"

"Of course. The law close after you?"

Reno shook his head. He struck a match and lighted the cigar. "The law don't know where I am. You seen Gage?"

"Not for a year. He comin' here, too?"

"I thought he'd be here now. Maybe I come faster. We hadda split to throw off some deputies."

"Put your horse in the stable. If Gage is on his way, he'll be here directly."

It had taken Gage longer. He had made a far wider circle than Reno and had missed the town, riding much too far south. But when he came to the river and saw the mountains in the distance, he realized he had gone past and turned about.

He came into Marshfield two days after Reno and went at once to Grady's saloon. Grady took him upstairs to Reno's room.

Ki visited every saloon in town over and over again and uncovered no evidence that either Reno or Gage had been in any of them. Marshal Hopkins's men did the same and found nothing.

Ki said to Jessie, "Maybe we're dead wrong and neither of them came here. Or if they did, they didn't stay."

"Maybe," she said. "There're a lot of houses in town. They could be in any one of them and never go near a saloon at all."

Of course that was true. "But it's not Reno's way," Ki said. "He likes excitement and gambling. How long is he going to stay cooped up in a room?"

She nodded. "A good question. You still think he's here?"

"No idea."

Jessie had supper with Scott. He had been ordered to Marshfield, he said, to talk to several witnesses. If a certain case went to trial, the government would need them to testify.

"But I'm thinking of leaving the marshal's office," he told her. "I may go east next year. I have friends who have offered me a position."

She was surprised. "I thought you enjoyed your work."

"Yes, I do. But sometimes I get tired and wish I were living like normal people. I'm on call night and day, you know."

"The east is so far away . . . Do you mean New York?"

"No. Chicago." He took her hand. "It all seems foolish to you, doesn't it?"

She laughed. "Maybe a better word would be 'unplanned.' "

Scott laughed with her. "Oh, I've given it a lot of thinking. I just haven't settled on any details. I've managed to save a lot of my pay . . ."

"How long has it been since you've been in the east?"

"Several years. Four, I suppose." He squeezed her hand. "But let's not worry about all that now."

He would be in town for several days, he said, and they'd have plenty of time to talk. After dinner they went to his room in the hotel . . . and made love.

Reno had less than two hundred dollars in his kick. He thought about taking the stage to, say, Kansas City, or some other large city where there would be plenty of opportunities to fatten his wallet.

But large cities made him nervous—they had better police forces and records, and tougher jails. He had been in one or two of them in past years and had been worked over by two ugly detectives when he didn't answer soon enough to suit them.

Two hundred dollars was not enough even to pleasure himself. And Gage had no more than he. Gage wanted to go back to the Mississippi, saying there were hundreds of towns along the big river, with merchants and maybe banks, ripe for plucking.

"We could hit us three—four stores ever' night and git away across the river. They'd never catch us."

Reno was not impressed. "How much you figger in them little stores?"

Gage shrugged. "Maybe a hunnerd. But it'd add up, Reno!"

It was small time. Reno shook his head. Gage would never get anywhere thinking small. What was needed was another like the Army payroll. He thought about that every day. All those stacks of cash!

Of course, if he really got down hard on his luck, he could always go back to Lassiter and get some. But he hated to. That secret money was his retirement cushion, against the days when he couldn't ride and shoot . . . That money was going to keep him in beans and firewood.

He discussed matters with Grady Harris. He said, "I don' want to let the summer get by. Any possibilities in this town?"

"Two'r three, I reckon. There's banks . . ."

"Not banks. What else?"

Grady smiled, fingering his stubbled chin. "The best is the stage."

Reno frowned. "Holdin' up a stage is—"

Grady held up his hand. "Lissen! Money comes here to the bank from out of town ever' Thursday."

"It comes here?"

"Yes. Well guarded. Five'r six guards."

Reno was very interested. "Where does the money come from?"

"Half a dozen small towns where there ain't no banks. The stage line makes a special trip. No passengers. Just horse guards and jaspers inside the stage."

Reno almost smiled. "How much we talking about?"

Grady shook his head. "I dunno. Nobody says. I s'pose it's different each time, but it must be a few thousand anyway. Or else they wouldn't be so many guards."

"What else?"

"Well, they bring it from them towns over west. They's only one road, so you can look it over, see for your own self."

"Ummmm. On Thursday . . ."

"That's right. The stage gets here about four in the afternoon ever'time I seen it. Stops at the Erskine National Bank."

Reno talked to Gage, telling him about the stage, and Gage was all for it.

"Five'r six guards, Reno, that's like the Army payroll. We c'n handle that." He sighed. "And money's goin' fast."

"You got to spend it all on girls?"

"What the hell else? Drinkin' just gives me headaches. We going to look at the stage run?"

"Yeah. I figger we'll act like a couple of drifters heading west. We'll pass by the stage and get a good look at it. Then we'll look for a place to hit it."

"All right. That's two days away."

★

Chapter 23

Jessie talked to the bankers in town while Ki roamed the saloons, asking questions when he could, but mostly listening. He heard nothing about Reno. Maybe the bandit wasn't in town at all. And if not, where was he?

Jessie discussed security with the bankers—who were glad to show her their precautions, and serve her coffee, and maybe rub up against her now and then. She pretended not to notice. Each manager showed her his plan—shotgun guards placed where they had every inch of floor space under view and clear fire paths to the doors. They could be seen by customers, yet had protection. She could find no fault with any of them. No bank in Marshfield had ever been robbed, and the managers took full credit for that fact.

One manager said to her, "No outlaw would be dumb enough to try this bank. He'd be cut down by shotgun cross fire in a second."

He was probably right.

Jessie spent the night with Scott Pelter, his last night before he had to leave. They talked, then made love, and she went to sleep in his arms.

In the morning she woke as he was slipping out of bed. "Where are you going?"

He turned and kissed her. "I must catch the early stage."

"Then I'll go with you to—"

"No." He embraced her. "Let's say our good-byes here, not in front of everyone at the depot. All right?"

She relented. "Very well . . ." He kissed her again, then got up and pulled on his jeans and boots. When he was dressed, he sat on the bed and looked down at her. "*Adios, Jessie . . .*" He hugged her, got up, and hurried out.

Reno and Gage rode out of town to the south after dark, without going through the main part of town. They circled around and came onto the road west an hour after first light.

They had blanket rolls behind their cantles and would have appeared to casual observers to be ordinary saddle tramps. Out of sight of the town, they got down and Gage made a fire to warm them. They had a long wait for the stage.

The day dragged past slowly. When a far-off dust cloud indicated the presence of a moving vehicle, they mounted and walked the horses along the road toward it. A stage and riders gradually appeared out of the haze. Reno saw three horsemen in front of the stage and two behind. A driver and shotgun guard were on the box.

As the stage came close, he saw that it was really a mud wagon, pulled by four horses. There were four riflemen inside, ten guards in all! The three in front herded Reno and Gage off the road as the stage passed. The outlaws halted and gazed after the group.

"Ten goddamn guards!" Gage said. "That ain't what Grady told us."

Reno scowled. "Maybe this was a big shipment."

173

"That's too many for us t'face unless we gets more men."

"That splits the take."

Gage shrugged.

They returned to town after dark, the same way they'd come, and Reno talked to Grady that night.

"We got a good look at the stage, and they was ten guards on it."

Grady was startled. "Ten?"

Reno nodded. "Too many for us two."

"Lemme ast some questions. There must've been something special about it."

Grady mentioned the ten guards when he went to deposit his saloon receipts at the bank and was told there had merely been an unusually large shipment of cash on board.

It might not happen again for months . . .

But it did.

Town Marshal Karl Hopkins was notified that another large shipment was due to come into Marshfield on the next Tuesday. Could he supply guards?

Hopkins replied by wire that he could not on such short notice, and suggested the shipment wait a week. There was no reply.

Hopkins told Jessie and Ki, "They're probably calling every lawman in the territory."

Ki asked, "Why won't they wait until it's safer?"

"Because of the loss of interest on the money," Hopkins said wearily. "You know how bankers are."

Grady Harris, tending his own bar, heard rumors of the special shipment and was able to confirm them. He told Reno, "They having trouble getting a passel of guards together. Too bad you and Gage ain't where you could be hired." He laughed. "Wouldn' that be a easy one!"

Reno was serious. "Where'd we have to go to get hired?"

174

"I dunno. Some one of them towns."

"Can't you find out?"

Grady was annoyed. "If I ast too many questions, folks is gonna wonder—after the holdup—why I wanted to know. I don'want them lawmen pokin' around here." He grinned at them. "They might find something."

Karl Hopkins heard the rumors also, on Sunday, and was worried that the Tuesday shipment had become common knowledge. "The more know about it, the more likely that some hardcase will hear of it, too."

"Where will the shipment start from?" Jessie asked.

"A town called Cedar Creek, about forty mile west." He looked at them hopefully. "You all ain't going that way, are you?"

Ki said, "We could . . . It's in a good cause."

"But will they listen to us?" Jessie said. "We don't know anything for sure. All we can give them is a rumor."

"Mention Reno," Hopkins said. "Tell 'em that we think he's in Marshfield, and if he's heard about money being shipped, he'll go after it."

"That's a good reason," Ki agreed.

Jessie nodded.

She and Ki set out while it was still dark, on Monday morning. It was an all-day ride to Cedar Creek, Hopkins had said, the road being what it was—up, down, and around. It had never been dragged. Too bad there wasn't another road, but no enterprising soul had pioneered one.

The weather was cool but not cold; spring was rushing upon them, and it would soon be summer. The sun came up behind them, streaking the sky. Jessie hoped they were not on a fool's errand.

About midday they saw the dust, and in another hour they came onto the mud wagon and six men. The driver and one man were on the box; two were inside and two mounted. Seeing Jessie and Ki, the driver halted the horses as the guards fingered their rifles. Then they relaxed, seeing Jessie come close.

She said to the driver, "Aren't you a day early?"

The burly driver nodded. He was an old-timer, with a scraggly beard and huge hands. "They sent us early. Who're you, miss?"

She smiled. "Karl Hopkins sent us. We were hoping you would change the day." Hopkins's name seemed to reassure them.

"You got a reason t'say that, missy?"

She nodded. "Reno Quant. We think he may be in Marshfield."

There was a definite reaction from the guards at the name. The driver said, "Damn me! Reno, huh?" He glanced at the horizon.

One of the horsemen said, "You figger we ought t'go back, Hap?"

The driver fiddled with the reins and pushed his battered hat back. "We's halfway there now . . ." He looked at her. "Reno got him a gang?"

"No. One man, as far as we know."

"One man, hey . . . ?" The driver squinted at the guards.

One said, "He could get more, couldn't he? I vote we go back."

Annoyed, the driver said, "We can't go back—or we don't get paid. We gotta take this damn strongbox to the bank. Now, let's get moving." He touched his hat to Jessie. "You all comin' along with us?"

"Yes, we are." She and Ki followed the wagon. The two mounted men led the way at a walk.

In the middle of the afternoon, as they came around a low, rocky hill, shots blasted from the rocks above them,

176

and the two lead horses stumbled and fell, halting the wheelers and the wagon.

The riflemen instantly returned fire and kept firing as the driver yelled. The men slid off their mounts and ducked behind the wagon. No one fired again from the hill.

Jessie and Ki spurred out of range to the left, both yanking out Winchesters. Was this Reno? If so, it was a poor ambush. He had fired too soon and had allowed the men to use the wagon as a fort. Maybe he had selected the hill in a hurry. She and Ki looked for targets in the rocks . . .

Then Ki noticed the tethered horses on the reverse slope and fired at them, but the range was too long.

Jessie yelled and pointed. The ambushers were running down the hill to the horses. She and Ki spurred to get closer, but the two outlaws galloped away to the north.

Apparently they did not wish to face eight rifles.

"Was it Reno?" the driver asked when they joined him. "Did you git a look at them?"

"They were too far," Jessie said. "By the time we got the binoculars out, they were gone."

Ki climbed the low hill on foot while the men chattered, all still excited at the shooting. When he reached the spot where the ambushers had fired at them, he shouted down, waving at them to come up.

Jessie, the driver, and two others hurried up the hill. Ki pointed silently.

The body of Gage Hindman lay on its face, arms sprawled. Ki moved the head gently. Gage had been shot in the neck and had died instantly.

Ki looked up at Jessie. "Now Reno's the only one left of the gang."

Everyone had been firing up at the hill; there was no way to know who had hit the outlaw. Someone said, "How much's he worth?"

"Five hundred at least," Ki said. "You all can share it."

They carried the body down the hill, wrapped it in a blanket, and put it in the wagon. One of the men rode around the hill and brought back Gage's horse, then they went on into town.

The body was delivered to the local undertaker, and the money box to the bank.

The driver came with Jessie and Ki to Karl Hopkins's office. Karl asked some questions. "Who was in charge of the mud wagon crew?"

"Well, not really nobody in charge," the driver said. "I figger I was in charge of the wagon, seein' how it's mine."

"You think they fired at you too soon?"

Ki nodded. "Too eager, maybe. But they played in bad luck, too."

"How d'you mean?"

"When the first shots came that hit the horses and stopped the wagon, everybody fired at once. I would have thought that almost impossible, but it happened. There was a hail of lead that hit that hill in and around those rocks. For a few minutes it sounded like a war. I'm only surprised the others didn't get hit, too."

"Maybe they did."

Jessie shook her head. "We found no other blood and no indication of a second wound. Ki and I went around the side, hoping to cut them off, but they got out fast. They didn't move like they were hurt."

"Gettin' out fast," the driver said, "that was the smartest thing they done all day."

Ki bought food at the nearest store, and they rode north out of Marshfield, on the trail of Reno and his companion. He must have recruited another gun, Ki said.

Marshfield was south of an extensive area of badlands that slashed across the country from west to east. The outlaws' tracks led directly to it, plain and clear.

Ki led the way, leaning down frequently to study the footprints. But when it began to get dark, he halted and slid down.

"Let's hope they don't split up. We don't want to follow the wrong man."

The next morning dawned misty and cool; the trail of the fleeing two was easy to follow. They did not split up, but they were traveling fast, evidently eager to cross the badlands as quickly as possible, which meant, Ki thought, that they had a destination in mind.

In an hour that morning, Ki found where they had spent the night, or part of it. They halted a moment at the spot, and Jessie said, "Why are they moving so fast? They're hours ahead of us."

"They're putting distance between them and the place Gage was shot. I doubt if they're even thinking of bushwhacking us. I'm sure they don't know we're here."

She gazed at the jumbled hills and shale cliffs. It would be easy for them to set an ambush . . . She said, "They can't be certain they won't be pursued."

Ki shrugged. "Maybe not . . ."

They went on, and Jessie followed Ki, the rifle cocked and ready, keeping a close watch on the hills and crevices beyond Ki, as he watched the trail.

Three hours went by, and Ki slid down to walk the horses for a spell. "They're cutting across this area to get to somewhere . . ." He looked at the cloudy sky. "I hope it stays this way—the tracks will last longer."

They walked the horses for miles . . . and did not reach the far side of the badlands till almost dark.

• • •

Ki got out the map and studied it, trying to locate their position. "It looks to me like they're heading straight for Denning."

Jessie frowned. "It's on the railroad."

"That's right."

"And that's the fastest way east or west out of this country."

Ki said, "Let's keep going. If they get on a train, we've lost them."

They had never been so close to Reno—he was almost within reach. They dared not travel too fast at night, for fear of running into him in the dark. Ki led, walking the horses for several miles before he halted.

"If they suspect we're here," he said, "they'll take measures to throw us off. Let's wait till morning."

Ki was up at first light, restless and itching to be on the way. Jessie had to hurry. He said, "I'm afraid the tracks will deteriorate if the sun comes out."

"Let's hope they stopped, too, last night . . ."

"They probably did. How hard can they push the horses?"

Ki lost the tracks toward midday but found them again a few miles farther on. The two outlaws were traveling in single file in brushy country, which made tracking easier.

In the afternoon they came to the shining rails. No town was visible in either direction. The tracks turned east to follow the rails.

"They're guessing," Ki said. "I would have turned west for Denning."

The rails made a long, gentle curve to the south, through one end of the badly eroded country that was torn by washes and arroyos, so that the rails crossed it on heavy wooden trestles.

The tracks disappeared in the tortured ground—the horses could not cross on the trestles—but they appeared again farther on. They led directly into the dusty town of Benton.

It was a burg the size of Havelock, with two hotels and a dozen saloons. They went at once to the depot. According to a weathered notice on the side of the building, there was no train in either direction for two days.

"We're in time," Jessie said. "Now where is Reno?"

★

Chapter 24

He was in the Congress Saloon, sitting alone, with a glass of beer before him, thinking about the near past. It was slightly unnerving, knowing that he was the only survivor of five people, in so short a time. True, Nate Tupper wasn't dead, but he might as well be, in prison for the rest of his life.

He could still see Gage Hindman rise up and flop instantly with a bullet in the throat. Gage had fallen and never moved. The bullets had pounded the rocks in front of them and ricocheted into the sky, a deadly, leaden hail that went on for five or ten minutes. It was impossible to decide if the men below at the wagon were determined or merely scared. But the result was the same . . .

And now he was far away from that miserable spot, in a ramshackle saloon, waiting for a train to take him east, and he had barely fifty dollars in his kick. He thought of going again to Lassiter, but no—it was just dumb luck. He had run into a spate of bad luck. It would change. It always had.

He knew a few of the right kind of people in Kansas City. He'd talk with them, and they'd help him recruit two or three likely men, and he'd be back in business. In maybe six months, he'd be in the chips and riding high again. Then, in a year or two he'd retire—just suddenly disappear. He'd get the money from the secret cache at Lassiter and go east for good and never look back.

That was the ticket. Never look back.

He got up slowly and stretched, feeling hungry. He'd go across the street and get a steak. He stepped out to the boardwalk and squinted at the pale sky.

Ki left Jessie at the livery and walked toward the center of town, to the near hotel. By the photographer's shop he halted—that was Reno, coming from the saloon! The outlaw glanced at the sky then was joined by a second man, in a blue coat, whose back was turned. The two talked, heads together for a minute, then Reno slapped the other's back jovially and went down the steps to the street. Blue Coat went into the saloon.

Ki walked to the center of the street and hurried toward Reno. The outlaw glanced at him, then slowed, scowling. He had seen this man before . . .

Ki said, "Reno Quant."

"What the hell you want!" Reno faced him, and Ki knew the outlaw had placed him.

Ki said, "I'm one of the two you tried to blow up at the old shack."

Reno went for his gun . . . and saw a silvery flash, felt the hit—then nothing. His body sprawled in the dirt; the pistol dropped from his lifeless hand.

Ki walked to the body and knelt. He recovered the *shuriken* from Reno's throat, wiped it on Reno's coat, and stood as people began to gather. He heard someone shout into the saloon, and a man with a star on his coat came out of the restaurant and frowned at the body.

Ki said, "It's Reno Quant, Deputy. There's probably something on him with his name on it."

183

"Reno! How'd he get dead?"

Ki showed him the *shuriken* and explained how it was used. As he spoke, he saw Jessie come from the stable and start toward them.

The deputy sent someone for the undertaker. Jessie came to Ki's side and looked down at the body with a sigh.

"So, it's over," she said.

He nodded to her, then saw her eyes dilate as she glanced over his shoulder. Her face changed instantly and Ki whirled. The man in the blue coat had come with others from the saloon—and Ki was astonished to see it was Scott Pelter!

Jessie said, "Scott!"

Scott stared at them, then suddenly turned and dashed back into the saloon. When they followed, they saw him running out into the alley, slamming the rear door.

Ki hurried into the alley and came back. Scott was on a horse, galloping out of town. Ki said to Jessie, "He was talking to Reno only a few minutes ago . . ."

Jessie felt cold. "He was in with Reno?"

"I'm afraid so. A man in his position was able to give Reno every sort of information over the years—for a cut of the profits."

She leaned on the building. "And we never suspected . . . God, we never once suspected . . ."

They informed the U.S. marshal at once concerning Pelter, and went on to San Francisco.

It was more than a month later that Ki showed Jessie a newspaper item. A former deputy marshal, Scott Pelter, had been recognized in Florida and had been shot resisting arrest. He had left no next of kin.

"It's water under the bridge," Ki said.

Jessie sighed deeply. "I don't want to believe any of it. None of it."

Watch for

**LONE STAR
AND THE SLAUGHTER SHOWDOWN**

139th novel in the exciting LONE STAR series
from Jove

Coming in March!